ALL THE WOMEN HE MET WERE BEAUTIFUL—AND ALL OF THEM WERE BAD TROUBLE

Pete had come home from Naval Reserve duty unattached and fancy free, looking for a woman. And he found:

Myra, the syndicate boss' wife—off limits to any man who wanted to stay alive.

Flo, who sheltered a "murder victim" till it was time for him to die again.

Serena, who could make love with no restraints—and kill in the same uninhibited way.

Clemi, who was willing to run away with him—after he helped her brother shoot his way out of jail.

He had learned in the Navy about handling high explosives—but no one had prepared him for the kind of dynamite that came in a well-stacked feminine package.

DEATH IS
MY SHADOW

EDWARD S. AARONS

MB

A MACFADDEN-BARTELL BOOK

A MACFADDEN BOOK

First printing...........................May, 1965
Second printing.................February, 1969
Third printing.....................January, 1971

THIS BOOK IS THE COMPLETE TEXT
OF THE HARDCOVER EDITION

Macfadden-Bartell Corporation
A subsidiary of Bartell Media Corporation
205 East 42nd Street, New York, New York 10017

Library of Congress Catalog Card Number: 57-12671

DEATH IS MY SHADOW

Chapter One

The doctor offered Byrum a cigarette, shoving the pack across his desk. It was hot in Los Angeles, but the air-conditioner that Stein had swindled from Government stores made his office comfortable. Stein was small and dark and totally unmilitary in his khakis, rumpled, sweaty, his beard a dark swath along his rounded jowls. His black eyes were friendly.

"Going home now, Byrum?" he asked.

"I'm through with the Navy," Byrum said. "Or it's through with me. Thanks for patching me up, Doc."

"Got a girl?"

"No. Yes. I don't know."

Stein smiled. "You sound confused. What's the trouble?"

"No trouble. I've never thought of Clemi as my girl. Perhaps she is."

"And home?"

"Oswanda, Louisiana."

"Under anesthesia, you spoke with a New York accent, Byrum. You talked about your gambling joint in Oswanda. About your father and the West Side docks and the troubles in the longshoreman's union."

Byrum looked at his cigarette. "Loose lip."

"Don't worry about it. Many patients have one under gas. Called Clemi yet?"

"No. I thought I'd surprise them all."

Dr. Stein sighed. "Sometimes surprises work in reverse. I'd suggest you telephone before you go home, Pete. You've got your discharge papers? No glory, no war now. No fanfare of trumpets, hey?" Stein laughed at his own words. "Just recalled to Reserve training duty and get hacked up."

"I'm grateful to be here."

"You've still got your dealer's hands," Stein said.

"That's my business," Byrum said. He was blunt, but he didn't want to be. He liked Stein. He was just itchy to be away from the hospital, on his way out into the sun and freedom from brass and regulations. "How did Capricorn make out in the fifth?"

"Won easily," Stein said. He took out his wallet and pushed a ten-dollar bill across to Byrum. Byrum took it.

"Now we're square. But I don't know how you figured it."

"Gambling is my business," Byrum said.

He stood on the hospital steps and breathed free air and looked at the sunshine and the date palms and the traffic going down the hill toward the city shrouded in smog. He hadn't telephoned Clemi yet. Or Steve. He still wore his rumpled khakis with the j.g. bar on his collar, the wings over his breast and a tropical tan won in the Gulf of Tonkin. He had been recalled for maneuvers in Southeast Asian waters, and he had resented it, angry about being yanked away from business and the life he had built since meeting Steve Dulaney. He thought of Stein's remarks. He had come a long way since that day they brought his father home from the West Side pier where the striking longshoremen had rioted and a thrown brick had hit John Byrum in the back of the head. He had gone fast and far, free at last, remembering the old man's words and adding a few dicta for himself. New York hadn't seen him since the war. He had gone with Steve Dulaney to Oswanda when they were both discharged, and Pelican Lodge was his home now.

He walked down the steps, feeling the constriction of the scars on his left side. Stein had wanted him to use a cane for the next month or two, but he couldn't see it. He had over eight hundred dollars in his pocket. In Oswanda, he had the *Firefly*, the convertible Buick, and a half interest in the Pelican worth at least fifty thousand dollars. He had Clemi and Steve Dulaney.

A long way from the jungles of New York.

He took a cab into town and at a certain corner on Sunset he got out and walked slowly, aware of the tightness of torn and mended muscles in his abdominal wall. After two blocks he turned into a small bar flanking a third-rate apartment hotel and walked through this into another room.

"Sit down," Ike Petersen said. "You're right on time. How's it feel to be a civilian again?"

"I never left it," Byrum said. He sat down across from Ike's desk. "You owe me three hundred and seventy-four dollars."

"Right."

"So pay me," Byrum said.

"Sure." Petersen opened a desk drawer and took out a thick wad of bills and counted them carefully, his big thumb going to his tongue to wet the bills, his bald head shining under the overhead light. "There you are, all of it. You're damned good at picking 'em."

"Thanks," Byrum said. He stood up. "It was nice doing business with you."

"Wait a minute. Have a drink, friend."

"I'm going home," Byrum said.

"I talked to Sam Carse about you," Ike said. "We could use a man like you right here. Pay you good, Pete."

"I have my own place."

"All yours?"

"I have a partner."

"Then sell out and stay here. Sam likes what I told him about you. There's big opportunities for a man like you. You're good, Pete."

"No, thanks. I like to be my own boss."

Petersen looked at him for a long moment, then shrugged. He looked sour and Byrum knew he was thinking of the organization, of the syndicate that gave orders to Petersen and really ran Petersen's bookie operation, which made Ike only a stooge and errand boy. None of that for him.

"See you around," he said, and left.

He had a two-hour wait at the airport for the turbo-jet to New Orleans. The August heat in Los Angeles was muggy and oppressive. Byrum lunched at the airport restaurant and waited patiently. He was not exceptionally tall, but he had muscular shoulders; he was thinner than he should be after the weeks in the naval hospital. Damned fool accident. He lit a cigarette, wishing he were home already. His recall to Navy flight duty couldn't have come at a more inconvenient time. Just when the Pelican was beginning to pay off, after all the sweat and toil and worry. Steve Dulaney was all right in most ways, but Steve was high-handed and apt to discharge business affairs with an aristocratic contempt for detail. And it was attention to details that made a business like the Pelican pay off.

They had met as Navy pilots long years ago, as youngsters, and he had taken an instinctive liking to the wild-tempered Louisianan. Meeting Steve Dulaney had changed the whole direction of his life.

At thirty, Peter Byrum was a long distance from the tenements and hard-fisted street life of a longshoreman's son. When his father was killed in that waterfront brawl, there had seemed to be only one direction for him. He had been hanging around Johnny Feers' bookie joint, running errands, acting as lookout for the game in the back room. The old man's death changed all that. He didn't remember his mother, and there had been no brothers or sisters—only the shabby apartment where the sun never touched the grimed windows, only the catch-as-catch-can life with the old man, who was sodden with liquor, lost in a daily routine of gut-busting labor and the solace of heavy drinking at night.

The day of the funeral, with the longshoreman's union providing clumsy pallbearers and paying expenses, Peter had locked the apartment door and never returned. He remembered the gray day, with rain sweeping over Manhattan. He remembered the raw words, the beery men who had put the old man to rest in the muddy grave. At eighteen, he saw the same gray road open to him.

There was a pay envelope in the old man's pocket, and a crumpled handful of bills collected by the pallbearers and thrust into his palm. He had not refused it. A total of forty-seven dollars and sixty-two cents. He had started out with that.

That night he asked Johnny Feers for a job as dealer. And got it. He spent two months learning every trick, honest and otherwise, of cards and dice, and enrolled at NYU to study law during the day. He took a small furnished room in a brownstone on Thirtieth. He learned what to wear and what to say and how to say it. The next year he transferred to Yale, wanting to get out of the city, away from Johnny Feers. In New Haven he set up his own game, not big enough to attract the attention of the big boys, but enough to pay tuition and continue his education. In two years Korea broke into flames and he enlisted rather than wait for the draft.

In New Haven he had made new friends, learned about boats, found a quick affinity in himself for the sea. He chose the Navy, got a commission and pilot's wings, and met Steve Dulaney. Instead of going back North after it was over, he accepted Steve's invitation to stay as long as he liked at the Dulaney place in Oswanda.

"It's no castle," Steve said, grinning. "More like a ruin describes it. The folks used to have a lot of land, but the blood and bank balance ran thin. Clemi and I rattle around in the old place like a couple of dice in a bowl. I ought to sell it, or turn it into an inn or something. But you'll see for yourself how the old Southern aristocracy lives on grits and beans."

"Who is Clemi?" Byrum had asked.

"Clementine, the kid sister. Just entering finishing school. You'll come, won't you?"

"I've got nothing to lose," Byrum said.

The place was a worse wreck than Steve had implied. But the location on a little private cove east of Oswanda Harbor, its proximity to oil rigs and shipyards booming down the coast, was interesting. Byrum was in no hurry to return North. Korea was behind him, a barrier between past and future. He had over ten thousand dollars in a New Haven savings account. When he looked at the decayed mansion and ruined stables, the old tennis court and formal gardens, he saw it as it could be. A high-class inn, with a gambling room in the upstairs ballroom, a small boat anchorage for fishing enthusiasts, a fine dining room. It was opportunity. He put his ten thousand dollars into it, along with Steve's wild enthusiasm.

None of it was easy. Sweat and backbreaking labor and discouragement went on seemingly forever before they opened. It cost money to remodel, more money to keep Sheriff Jergens quiet about the roulette wheels and faro games, money to advertise quietly what the Pelican had to offer. The Dulaney name was a help in monied circles. Maury Harris, the Dulaney attorney, kept the books and accounts and fended off the law.

Only Clemi objected. She had been a gangling kid, soft-eyed, towheaded, freckled. "Yes, an inn for tourists, a fishing lodge, tennis courts, a fine dining room. Why are the wheels necessary?"

"Honey, don't trouble your little noggin about it," Steve said. "Pete knows what he's doing."

"Of course he does," she said. "But do you?"

A silent feud went on between Clemi and Byrum the first years, but she wasn't around much, usually off at boarding school in Atlanta, and when no trouble developed, her lack of comment seemed to be acceptance.

Byrum got up from the bench in the airport waiting room and walked toward the telephone booths. The muggy heat made him feel as if his lungs were filled with water. All those weeks in the hospital had left him a little less than he had been. He was going home from the unde-clared wars in Southeast Asia, the tedium and monotony of Naval patrol duty there. And you'd still be out there, he thought, worrying about receipts and figuring how to make the dining room pay more, if it hadn't been for that hot-rod jet pilot coming in with a flame-out, quartering into the wind to crash on the flight deck in a pile of screaming steel and bursting flames.

You didn't give it a thought when it happened. You heard Callahan screaming in that mess of burning steel and gasoline and you were running across the tilting flight deck to drag the ensign out of the jammed cockpit. Then the .50's in the wing cannon cut loose, fired by a short circuit in one of the gutted controls, and slugs came spraying across the deck. One of them hit you in the side and another grazed your leg and picked you up and threw you down. But you still managed to drag Callahan out of the plane and away from the explosion that ended it all for you until you woke up between white sheets, gauze and ointments plastered all over your side and that terrible ache in your belly.

All the resentment you felt about being put back into uniform was gone and you were only aware of the fact that you might die. And nobody wrote to you and you didn't write yourself and you were sore at the whole world until Dr. Stein snapped you out of it.

Byrum went into one of the phone booths and sat down.

It took a long time to get through to Oswanda, and his anticipation grew. Steve would be surprised. Clemi would be pleased. The stiffness he felt all through his left side didn't matter so much, suddenly. He was going home and everything would soon be the same again.

He spoke to a strange desk clerk at the Pelican's switchboard, a heavy-voiced man who seemed surprised at a call from the West Coast for Steve Dulaney.

"Mr. Dulaney is not available, Mr.—uh—"

"Byrum. Peter Byrum. Hunt him up, will you?"

There was a long, mysterious moment of humming silence.

"I'm sorry, Mr. Dulaney isn't here," the strange voice said. "If you care to leave a message, Mr. Byrum . . ."

"Let me speak to Miss Clemi."

"I'll see if she's on the premises."

Frowning, he waited in the stifling phone booth. Patsy McHugh had always handled the desk at the Pelican Lodge. Maybe Patsy was ill, or maybe Steve had finally let him have the vacation he always wanted. Over the p.a. system in the airport waiting room came the announcement that Flight 202 for New Orleans was boarding. He had six or seven minutes yet.

"Hello?"

"Clemi," he said happily. "This is Pete."

"Pete! *Pete?*" Her voice was shocked, not at all what he had expected. "Where on earth are you?"

"L.A.," he said. "And heading home."

"Here?"

"Where else? I'm a free man again. A civilian. Where can I get in touch with Steve?"

"Pete," she said. "It's really you." She laughed softly, but with a tight edge of dismay. "Didn't you get my letters? Are you all right?"

"I've been in the hospital. I'll give you the gruesome details when I see you. I'll be in New Orleans late tonight, probably sleep over and get my boat out. Maybe you can arrange to have the *Firefly* ready for me, Clemi. I'll stop off and pick her up and sail in."

"*Why* didn't you write?" she demanded. "I wrote to you; I told you all about it—"

"The mail went astray. What is it?" he asked. "Is anything wrong?"

"Everything. Pete, you can't—you can't come back here." She spoke breathlessly. "I can't explain now, over the phone. We've had a lot of trouble here. Can I meet you in New Orleans?"

"What's wrong?" he asked again.

"Listen, don't telephone again. Don't let anyone else know you're coming. Did you phone anyone else?"

"No, but—"

"Then don't. I want to talk to you first. You should have gotten my letters. I wondered why you didn't write and I thought it was just the slow mails or something. Oh, Pete—"

He listened to a strange soft sound in the receiver. She was crying.

"Clemi, for God's sake—"

There was a pause. "Pete, if you knew how much we needed you here—and you're coming home at last—"

"Clemi, tell me what the trouble is."

"I can't. Not over the phone. Meet me somewhere, Pete. With the *Firefly*, before you see anyone. Don't try to contact Steve; you won't find him. Meet me tomorrow at Kettle Creek. Make it four in the afternoon. I'll drive down Kettle Road and meet you at the old dock there—"

"Clemi?"

She hung up.

Byrum stared at the disconnected, humming receiver.

Over the p.a. system came a second announcement urging passengers to board Flight 202 at once. He opened the door to the telephone booth and then he heard the operator's querulous voice, tiny and faraway in the receiver he still held in his hand. He hung up on the metallic sound.

What was it Dr. Stein had said? *Sometimes surprises work in reverse.*

Byrum picked up his bag and hurried toward the wide door and the ramp to the waiting, shining plane.

Chapter Two

Alton Thayer pushed his wheelchair angrily across his office in Pelican Lodge. His office now, he reflected. It had taken a long time and the board in New Orleans had put a lot of pressure on him to prove his ability to take over this operation. In a way, Thayer considered, he had been strenuously tested, proving that a man didn't have to have the use of his legs to run a plant like this.

Rudge lounged easily just inside the office doorway. "Byrum called from L.A.," Rudge said. "I plugged him in to Clemi Dulaney and listened to some of it, but then one of the guests began yakking over the desk and I had to quit."

"Is Byrum coming back?"

"Yes. Maybe tomorrow."

"Miss Dulaney doesn't know you overheard the call?"

"I think not, Al."

Thayer sighed. Night had fallen over the Gulf, and far away through the tall windows of what had once been the master suite in the Dulaney mansion, he saw the flickering red flares of oil rigs low on the horizon.

"We'll talk to Clemi," Thayer decided. "Go get her."

"You think that's smart, Al?"

Thayer spoke irritably. "I think. You work. Go on."

Rudge nodded and moved away, a tall blond man, handsome in a brutal way, with sloping muscular shoulders under his gabardine jacket. Thayer had no illusions about him. Rudge represented the New Orleans syndicate that wanted this operation. Rudge was here to watch and report on what was done. There was a policy against violence these days, but Rudge had all the violence of a stick of dynamite ready to explode. But today the business was run quietly, keeping out of the press, without the bloody internecine fights of the early years. Thayer had grown up in those years, grown big and powerful, until this parish was his and he had the confidence of the hard-eyed men who met biweekly in the board room in New Orleans. It was the center of the web, Thayer thought, where punk amateurs like Pete Byrum and Steve Dulaney either came hat in hand to yield a share of their profits, or went down in disaster.

He reached across the desk to pick up the phone and call Myra, then yanked his hand away with anger, feeling hate and humiliation like sour bile in his throat. His spinal injury had paralyzed him from the waist down, but it wasn't that which made everything wrong. *Myra and Steve, Myra and Steve.* The linking and the coupling went through his mind like a dark litany.

Thayer was big even in his wheelchair, with iron-gray hair and meaty shoulders and a look of strength in his square features. He was dressed immaculately for dinner, but he wouldn't go down into the dining room tonight. He would eat in the big Spanish-type house he had bought on the Knoll. Myra would be there, silent and beautiful, cold and hating. He could force her to do what he wanted, give what he asked. Anything but love. Well, he had her for his wife, and by God, he would keep her. Once Steve Dulaney was out of the way . . .

The board was watching that, too, he thought. Maybe they're laughing about it around their cigars, discussing it.

"I hear Al Thayer's having trouble with his fancy society wife."

"Yeah. The Dulaney boy beat his time."

"If he can't control his own wife—"

"—then he can't control the operation, either."

And somebody, maybe Markley, would say, *"Give Al a chance. Another month. He got the Pelican. See what he does with it."*

"Is Rudge reporting?"

"Rudge is all right. He's watching it."

"But Al Thayer—first, he gets in that damned car accident, cracks his spine, gets stuck in a wheelchair . . . Hell, he used to be good."

"We don't need mugs now. We need businessmen, gentlemen. Al is in the Pelican. We'll just watch."

"But his wife and that Dulaney boy—"

"We'll wait and see."

Thayer pushed the imaginary sounds and hard faces from his mind, swept the wheelchair around with a powerful shove of arms and shoulders, and rolled to the window again. The heat was a smothering blanket over the Gulf Coast. He stared at the black expanse, watching the flickering flares of the oil rigs, hearing the sound of dinner music begin in the dining room below. Then it happened again, the rain and the water sluicing off the windshield of the big yellow Cadillac while he drove, thinking about Myra and her old man, the way the old man hated him but accepted the dough to keep his business going, the way the whole deal had been arranged and Myra had said she would marry him. He had played it smart, boxing in the old man, squiring Myra around town, buying out half the shops on Canal Street for her. The rain, the clack of windshield wipers, the other car careening crazily along the highway, the flare of lights, the brakes, the smooth, deadly swish of locked wheels skidding on wet asphalt. Blinding light. Pain too wild to endure, red flames, turning over and over into the water of the canal alongside the *cheniere* . . .

Thayer shivered, sweating, and looked down at his body helplessly chained to the wheelchair. Myra had married him anyway. And he had the Lodge now. Nobody could take Myra or the Pelican away from him. The board trusted him. Everything would be all right.

Rudge came back into the office.

Clemi Dulaney walked ahead of him, a touch of anger in her hazel eyes. There were red marks on her forearm where Rudge had put his hands on her.

"Sit down, Miss Dulaney."

"I'm busy. There's some difficulty in the kitchen—"

"Don't worry about it. Please make yourself comfortable." Thayer's voice was deep, persuasive, cordial. "We have something to talk over."

He watched the graceful way she seated herself across from the desk. Rudge lounged, unsmiling, waiting. The girl was in her early twenties, with long legs and good hips. She wore her summer cotton dress with Myra's manner, and Thayer reflected that these two were much alike. They belonged to a class that had always seemed unattainable to him. Good families, breeding, education. The blood had sickened in many areas of the South, but not in this girl, or in Myra, although the weakness was there in Steve Dulaney, like a deep-running, fatal flaw. He remembered how he had regarded these people in his early years, shrimp-fishing in the Gulf, sweating and breaking his guts for a few stinking bucks. And then the rum-running began, with Grog Mossan as the boss, and after a time he himself became boss, with a fleet of fast boats running like ferries on schedule to Cuba, Jamaica, and all through the Caribbean. Years of red violence and sudden death. But he had survived. He was high up in the echelons of the new order now. A gentleman.

"Well?" Clemi asked impatiently.

"I want to know about Pete Byrum," Thayer said. He made his voice paternal. "We know he telephoned you just now from L.A. Is he coming back to Oswanda?"

"Does that worry you?"

"Not at all. We can arrange some satisfactory agreement with Mr. Byrum. Last year we were not interested enough in the Pelican to make an issue out of it. But now the situation has changed. Today it is organization that realizes profit. We can convince Mr. Byrum to be reasonable."

Clemi said thinly, "You look worried, though."

"When is he coming back?"

"When he gets here."

"Miss Dulaney, your attitude is not very co-operative."

"Why should it be?" she said flatly. "You've forced your way in here and I know what you've done to my brother."

"Are you planning to meet Byrum somewhere?"

"Yes."

"Good. Now tell me where and when you will meet him."

Clemi was silent, her eyes meeting Thayer's pale gaze directly. She was afraid of Alton Thayer, but nothing could induce her to show it. She had stood up alone against him for over a month now, with Steve gone. She knew Thayer for what he was—a bloody-handed hoodlum masquerading behind his façade of quiet business manners. This was what she had tried to warn Pete about long ago. Pete was strong enough to take on Thayer. Or was he? When she looked into Thayer's cold eyes she wasn't sure of anything. She stood up.

"Miss Dulaney, you have not answered my question."

"I don't intend to."

"I would like to do this in a friendly fashion, Miss Dulaney."

"I won't help you trap him."

Thayer smiled. "Trap? Nonsense. We don't do business that way."

She turned to the door. "Good night, Thayer."

"Rudge?" Thayer said quietly.

Rudge twitched his shoulders away from his lounging posture in the doorway. Beyond him, the wide corridor led to the graceful, carpeted stairs curving down to the main lobby. Music drifted up from the dining room, voices laughed and glasses clinked in the bar. Clemi started past Rudge.

"Excuse me," she said.

Rudge laughed. His big hand closed on her arm, whirled her around with sudden, shocking violence. Clemi's eyes opened wide and she started to speak, but before she could say anything, Rudge slapped her with his left hand, hard, then brought his hand back in a blow that knuckled her open mouth.

Clemi fell back against the wall, staggered. The pain numbed her. She stared at Rudge with unbelieving eyes. Rudge hit her again and a thin sound came from between her clenched teeth. A trickle of blood showed at the corner of her mouth. As Rudge lifted his hand again, Thayer spoke.

"Enough, Charles. She will help us now, I think. We are in earnest, Miss Dulaney. Tell us about Byrum."

"No," she whispered.

"Close the door, Rudge," Thayer said.

Rudge closed the door.

"Now, Miss Dulaney."

Rudge moved toward her like a big, cruelly smiling cat.

The sky was like brass over the Gulf Coast, yellow and streaked with lavender over the sea, blinding gold-white over the swamps. Byrum sprawled on the small forward deck of his boat and felt the heat like a hammer blow on the back of his neck. The dampness made his field glasses fog when he lifted them to study the narrow lane and the causeway that led out from the mainland. He pushed the gun back into the shadow from the low cabin. The oily metal of the Colt felt hot and unpleasant to the touch.

The narrow channel had barely admitted the *Firefly*. Ahead, where giant swamp oaks dripped moss over the tidal water, the shadows looked cool and dark, like a damp cave. But the boat wouldn't have floated there. Remembering the tide, he figured he had less than an hour before he would have to back out.

Clemi should have been here an hour ago.

He shifted position to ease the ache in his side. He watched a heron flap like a dirty gray ghost through the primeval wilderness beyond the channel. Something made a clicking noise in the muddy lagoon where the salt-water creek dissipated itself, and the boat lifted and fell as some disturbance created an echoing swell. He looked back across the glare of swamp and sea and saw a dirty-white fishing boat pass toward the channel buoy that marked the entrance to Oswanda's harbor, a mile or more to the west. The chugging of the one-lung diesel aboard the shrimper drifted in rhythmic pulses across the hot, brassy air. He did not think he could be seen from that direction.

Again he lifted the field glasses and studied the rutted lane and causeway where Clemi would have to come to meet him. He thought briefly that all this was foolish, that she had given way to some unknown alarm far beyond whatever the situation called for. But Clemi had always been calm, anything but given to edgy nerves.

Byrum stood up, feeling sweat run off him, soaking his white singlet, his khaki uniform trousers. The dusty causeway and the road across the swamps were empty. Clemi was not in sight. The sun blinded him and he closed his eyes against the hot glare. Then he looked again at the haze of brassy sky and blue sea.

The air was still, tasting of metal, rank with the smell of tidal mud. The sound of a boat motor came from the seaward end of the channel where he had moored, and Byrum stood up, tall and thick-muscled, his scars twinging as he straightened on the narrow deck. The white fishing boat he had seen passing to seaward had swung into Kettle Creek behind him. The shrimper nosed into view astern, dirty and battered, the diesel chugging laboriously in the heat. Byrum looked at his watch. After four in the afternoon. The tide was going out. The channel astern was no more than fifteen feet wide and the fishing boat adequately blocked his passage.

Byrum moved on silent sneakers around the cabin and stepped down into his cockpit to face the other boat across his transom. The fisherman had a high blunt bow and a square cabin and a pulpit extending far out forward. He could see no name painted on her. Dimly he made out the figures of two men through her dirty windshield. They did not come alongside. The boat halted, the bow wave rocking the *Firefly* in the narrow channel, and hung there, diesel idling against the outgoing pull of the tide.

Nobody stepped out on deck to hail him.

He was about to call to ask them to let him clear out when sound came from the road he had been watching. A car was approaching, moving fast, red dust boiling up in a long, trailing cloud behind it. Low-slung and racy, a bright red jewel glaring in the hot evening sunlight. It was a Jaguar, and a man and woman rode in it.

Uneasiness moved cool fingers along the nape of his neck. The car was still a few minutes away. The fishing boat was twenty feet astern. He hailed the boat.

A man stuck his head out of the cabin.

"I'm leaving," Byrum said. "Would you mind pulling out to let me go by?"

The man grinned. "Yeah, we'd mind. You got a date here, Byrum."

Byrum was still. The fisherman knew his name. Uneasiness changed to alarm as a second man came out of the cabin, carrying a shotgun in the crook of his arm. He stepped and spat over the stern of the dirty white boat, looking at the approaching car.

Byrum turned to study the approaching car. The woman in it wasn't Clemi Dulaney. Abruptly he turned and walked forward around the cabin to the Colt .45 he had left on the deck. He straightened with the gun in his hand, and the fisherman with the shotgun called across the channel:

"Drop it, Byrum. Right now, heah?"

The shotgun was pointed dead-center at him. The man was short and chunky, grizzle-headed under his peaked blue cap, and his chambray shirt was stained dark with sweat. The second man, leaning on the rail and watching with amusement, was taller, dirtier.

"Into the drink, Byrum," he said quietly.

Byrum spoke thinly. "What's this all about?"

"You just behave nice and polite, Yankee boy, and nothing happens at all. Now drop the gun. Easy-like, over the side."

The man with the shotgun said, "I ain't fooling, mister."

The sunlight made a shiny ribbon of light on the shotgun. Byrum dropped his Colt over the side. It made a small splash in the murky channel water. The man with the shotgun chuckled. "Now you just talk nice when the folks get here."

The Jaguar came bouncing over the rutted road off the causeway. There was a rickety wooden landing at the bank of Kettle Creek, a leaning pier on thin pilings thrust into the bottom ooze. The road ended here, where Byrum had tied up. He squinted into the sun at the man and woman in the red car, and then it stopped, front wheels just short of the ramshackle dock.

The woman had been driving and she got out first. Byrum

looked back at the fishing boat and saw that the man with the shotgun still covered him, but the other had gone into the cabin to nose the fishing boat closer alongside. He looked again at the woman.

Serena Thayer. More than a year ago, Byrum had quietly asked her never to come to the Pelican again. He did not want her patronage. She had been angry and vituperative then, all the false femininity drained out of her.

She smiled now. "Pete, darling. Welcome home."

Byrum watched Serena Thayer pick her way daintily across the rickety pier toward his moored boat. She was a tall, thin girl, too angular to be appealing in her white shorts and pinkly feminine blouse. Her breasts were small and pointed and arrogant under the thin silk. Her dark red hair was curled short, combed severely back from a widow's peak. She had her brother's wide mouth and pale gray eyes that looked with contempt at a world inferior to what she deserved. Mexican silver jingled on her thin wrists.

The fisherman with the shotgun gestured casually. "Talk nice to the lady, Byrum."

"Where is Clemi?" he demanded.

"Oh, really now." Her voice was a mock-simper. She stood looking down at him, one hip askew. "We've been waiting anxiously for you to come back, Petey. Alton and I have looked forward to it. Didn't Clemi tell you?"

"Where is she?" he asked again.

"Weeping in frustration, I'm sure, because Alton heard her talk to you on the extension phone at the Pelican."

"What was your crummy brother doing there?"

"Don't be silly, darling. Al has every right to be at the Pelican. Poor Clemi really didn't tell you anything, did she?"

"Suppose you do that," Byrum said. His voice was low and dangerous. He was angry now.

Then the man got out of the Jaguar and walked to the pier to stand beside Serena Thayer. Byrum knew him. Charles Rudge. He had broken Rudge's nose a year ago in a fight on the tennis courts behind the Pelican. Rudge wore a yellow sports shirt and cocoa-brown slacks and open-toed sandals with silver buckles.

"Don't waste time with him, Serena. Alton wants to see him right away."

Serena laughed. "The poor lamb is so confused."

"Al will straighten him out."

The tide gurgled around the *Firefly's* bow, sliding through the channel on its way to the Gulf. The gray heron came back, flapping awkward wings to settle on a dead pine farther up the channel. The beat of wings found an answering beat of alarm in Byrum's pulse. He didn't like the look on Rudge's cold, handsome face, the smile on Serena Thayer's lips, or the queer light that shone in her intense, over-large gray eyes.

Thayer and his sister had tried to move in on the Pelican a year ago—first with apparently legitimate offers to buy, then with threats, finally with overt violence that had wrecked the dining room in a crude hoodlum riot. Byrum had been forced to close the gambling rooms until Sheriff Jergens gave him the nod again. He and Steve had fought back, and won.

At the time Byrum had been recalled to duty, Thayer apparently had forgotten the Pelican. But it wasn't over.

Byrum stared at Serena Thayer's thin, mincing figure and his anger deepened.

"Poor Peter," Serena said. "Things have changed, you know. It's too bad you had to be away when it all happened."

"When what happened?"

"Al will explain everything. Darling, don't look so angry. It really isn't as bad as all that."

"Thayer and I don't have anything to talk about," Byrum said. "We settled all that long ago. He can't buy or bulldoze his way into the Pelican."

"Oh, but he has," she simpered.

Byrum looked at her quietly. He felt dismay and the hot prodding of anger at the way he had been boxed in here. Long ago, he had known he was taking a calculated risk in opening the gambling room in the Pelican as a solitary venture, without contact or subservience to New Orleans. His white singlet was sticking to his ribs, sweat running down his khaki trousers. He looked at the squat fisherman on the boat alongside and saw the hot sunlight glinting on the oily barrel of the shotgun.

Serena still stood on the pier looking down at him, the same bony hip askew. Her lipstick was too heavy on her wide mouth and although she was smiling, he could not fathom the hot look in her gray eyes.

"You see," she said, "Steve Dulaney sold out his shares in the Pelican. To Alton. Al is your new partner, Petey."

"I don't believe you," Byrum said flatly.

"Of course not. I didn't expect you to. That's why we arranged for you to see Al before you did anything silly."

"I'll see Steve and Clemi first."

"That may be difficult," she said, relishing her words.

"Why?"

"Steve Dulaney is in jail. He's been charged with murder."

Chapter Three

Rudge looked big and brutal, a blond giant of a man, standing beside Serena Thayer. He was a man with external polish, an Oxford accent, a taste for strange women and brutality. Sunlight glinted on Rudge's watch on his thick wrist as he waved a hand.

"Take it easy, Byrum. Lots of things have changed here. No need to get excited right now, though. Alton is willing to talk a deal."

"Who is Steve supposed to have killed?" Byrum asked. His voice was harsh in the stifling, humid air.

Rudge looked amused. "A man named Adam Fahey. Just a loafer off the docks. Steve lost his head and slugged him a bit too hard. Steve was always high and mighty around Oswanda. But times have changed. You can't go around killing people with impunity, old boy."

"What was the fight about?"

Rudge smiled, showing big white teeth. "Nobody knows. Steve was drunk, that's all."

"You're lying. Steve doesn't get drunk."

"Alton will convince you. He has the partnership papers, a receipt for sixty thousand dollars paid to Dulaney. Thayer owns an even fifty per cent of the Pelican now, Byrum. Get used to the idea. Thayer is your partner."

"Steve wouldn't sell out to New Orleans," Byrum said.

There was bright malice in Rudge's tawny eyes. "The sooner you swallow the idea, the better things will be for everybody. There's nothing you can do for Steve Dulaney. And nothing you can do to get rid of Alton. Thayer's been running the Pelican for a month now, while Steve is in jail waiting trial. As soon as you make up your mind to it, we'll all get along. That's why we're here. We figured it would be best to talk to you first."

"Pete, darling," Serena said, "it's not as bad as all that. Alton will be quite fair to you."

Byrum was aware of the hot sun settling below the live oaks farther up the channel. The heron perched as if carved of stone on the dead pine. He heard the gurgle of the tide around the boats, the slap of current against the *Firefly*'s bow. Nothing was what he had expected. He had come home unarmed, with no warning except Clemi's anxious words. He found it hard to believe that Steve was in jail, charged with the murder of an obscure waterfront loafer. And even harder to believe that Steve, who had held Thayer and the New Orleans people in complete contempt, would sell out his partnership behind his back.

He looked at the two fishermen on the boat, at Rudge, at Serena Thayer. Anxiety for Clemi suddenly touched him. If Steve was in jail, then Clemi had been alone against this crowd. They had kept her from meeting him here and had come in her place. Why?

His anger deepened. Abruptly he stepped down into the cockpit of his boat.

"Byrum," Rudge said.

He looked up at the big blond man.

"We want you to be reasonable. Don't blow your stack. Alton wants to do business with you. He'll buy your half of the Pelican. He's got a good offer ready for you."

"The Pelican's not for sale," Byrum said.

He stabbed the starter button and the *Firefly*'s engine suddenly throbbed with life. Rudge gestured to the two men in the boat. The short, stubby one with the shotgun stood back. His taller friend jumped into the *Firefly*'s cockpit as Rudge stepped down onto the forward deck. Serena Thayer watched, smiling, her mouth open and glistening.

"Shut it off," Rudge said.

Byrum reached to cast off the line. The fisherman swung a fist like a ham. Byrum ducked, caught his arm and twisted. The man fell grunting against the engine hatch. Rudge swung around the cabin and jumped down, grinning.

"If you don't want to do business one way, Byrum, we'll teach you another."

"Get off my boat."

Rudge snapped off the ignition. The motor coughed and died. Byrum put his back to the cabin hatch, facing the three men. The fisherman with the shotgun had come aboard, too. Serena remained on the dock, watching with avid eyes.

"All right," Rudge said. "Go to it."

The man with the shotgun put it down and advanced with short steps, arms spread. The boat rocked with their weight. The thought came to Byrum that they could do anything to him in this deserted place and no one would ever know. He struck hard, blindingly fast.

The short man fell back. His companion jumped, and Byrum felt his bad leg twinge as he twisted. Something crashed down on the back of his neck and he found himself on hands and knees on the deck. The yellow sky reeled overhead. He climbed up, and Rudge moved in lightly, clipped Byrum's jaw, swung again and missed as Byrum moved under the blow and struck back. Rudge bounced against the side of the cockpit, shook his head, came in again. The two fishermen crowded with him. Byrum did the best he could. The taller of the two fishermen reeled to the stern and folded over the transom, vomiting from Byrum's fist in his belly. There were no rules. Byrum kicked and chopped and swung, but the odds were too great.

Land and sea and sky blurred. His bad leg caved in and he sprawled on the deck, between the engine hatch and the forward cabin. A boot slogged into his ribs. His lungs were on fire, his vision blurred by sweat and blood. He was being beaten into insensibility. He shook his head, tried to clear it. Rudge reached down and grabbed his hair and yanked his head back, smiling.

"Byrum, you're stupid. You know that?"

He tried to get up and one of the fishermen put his foot in his back and shoved. Pain surged through him. He heard someone shout from the fishing boat and lifted his head in dull surprise. There was a third man aboard the other vessel. He saw the man's shape dimly, slim and wavering, a narrow, ratty face with frightened eyes, mouth open, a bottle glinting in the man's hand.

Rudge gave a shout of anger. "Get that fool below, Rafe!"

The tall fisherman cursed. "Hell's shingles, he was stoned a minute ago."

"You should have dropped him first."

"We couldn't have made it here in time, if we did."

The skinny man in the checked cotton shirt was drunk and unaware of anything but alarm at what he had seen. The other two grabbed him and hustled him below in the fishing boat.

Rudge prodded Byrum with the toe of his silver-buckled sandals. "Byrum, did you see him?"

"I . . . Who?"

Rudge stood spread-legged, staring down at him. He sucked at his lower lip and looked up at the dock where Serena stood watching and shrugged. Byrum dragged air into his burning lungs. There was darkness all around him, and from high over his head he heard Rudge speak again.

"This was lesson number one, Byrum. Alton Thayer wants to talk to you. When you think you can crawl, start crawling to him. Don't try to walk. Crawl. Maybe then he'll give you a break."

Byrum heard him as if through a vast distance. The *Firefly* rocked as the two fishermen climbed back into their own boat. Rudge's footsteps returned to the sagging pier where Serena Thayer waited. The fishing boat started up and backed out of the channel. A few moments later he heard car doors chunk shut as Rudge and the girl got into the Jaguar and drove away.

He did not move. He felt broken. There was a metallic and ugly taste of fear in the back of his throat. He lived with his pain, waiting for it to subside. A gull screamed and water lapped against the boat's side. The afternoon sun burned him without mercy and at last forced him to sit up painfully, clinging to the engine hatch to haul himself to an upright position.

Long shadows reached from the swamps inland. There was a small silver flask in his bag, and he dug it out with stiff fingers. The liquor burned when he tilted the flask. Slowly he began to feel better. The causeway to the mainland was empty.

Clemi wasn't coming. . . .

The tide was almost at ebb. Only inches of water remained under the *Firefly*'s bottom as he backed away from the landing. Byrum thought of trying to retrieve the gun from where he had dropped it over the side, but gave it up. His leg troubled him as he sat behind the wheel.

It was a forty-minute run to the Pelican, and Byrum finished the bourbon on the way. He used an inland channel between the outer barrier islands and the mainland, keeping the engine at half throttle. It was five o'clock when he cleared Sand Key and picked up the nun buoy at the main channel entrance. The white fishing boat was long out of sight.

Other fishing boats were tied up at the long wharf that prodded the waterway. Beyond the wharf were tin-roofed sheds with heat waves shimmering off the corrugated metal, a wide landing and the town square, lined with dusty green oaks. The earth looked like pulverized brick, dusty-red. The white jailhouse made Byrum squint when he glimpsed it going by the harbor entrance. He wondered if Steve Dulaney was really in there. Then the Pelican Lodge appeared beyond a long green point of land where Oswanda's aristocracy had their homes. The Lodge was a Southern colonial on a small knoll overlooking a private cove and anchorage.

A lot of sweat, energy and grief had gone into remodeling the tumble-down ancestral Dulaney home. Byrum had had to learn carpentry, masonry, house painting, plumbing and every other conceivable craft in order to economize. But for the last two years the ledgers had been in the black. The Pelican had caught on, not only as a tourist inn and fishing center, but as a place for an evening's dinner, dance and, if desired, a fling at the wheels and games upstairs. It had a reputation for honesty that Byrum had labored hard to achieve.

Byrum throttled down the engine and the *Firefly* eased beyond the inn's anchorage and around a second low point of land. A small cove and dock and boathouse appeared. The sun blinded him as he nosed in to the landing. For privacy, Byrum had long ago chosen for his own the original boathouse that came with Dulaney's estate. It was detached from the hotel by the wooded point, and not for use by the guests. He moved stiffly as the bow nudged the dock and jumped ashore.

Nothing seemed changed. He picked up his bag and limped up the wooden stairs that lifted along the side of the white-painted boathouse to a gallery and his front door. His apartment held two rooms, a bath, and a tiny kitchenette. The windows had been opened, but the stale smell of six months of disuse greeted him when he entered.

His image in the living-room mirror was a shock. His khaki trousers were torn at the knee, his singlet was blood-stained and streaked with oil. There was a cut over one dark eyebrow and a rivulet of blood had crusted along the line of his jaw. One eye was going to puff up very soon.

Ten minutes later he stood under a hot shower that eased his bruised muscles. Nothing had been changed in the apartment, and before entering the shower he had found his .38 Colt automatic and put it on the washbasin within easy reach.

He felt better after the shower, and he was almost dressed, selecting dark blue gabardine slacks and a white shirt and woven moccasins, when Clemi called from the doorway.

"Pete? Is that you?"

He came out of the bedroom and saw her standing just inside the entrance. Suddenly everything about his homecoming changed for him.

Clemi was tall, with Steve's blond hair. She had the Dulaney hazel eyes, good cheekbones, wide forehead. Her hair was long, with a sleek wave to the nape of her neck, and her skin was a golden tan against her white sharkskin dress. A red belt cinched the dress around her slim waist and emphasized the womanly flare of her hips. Her hazel eyes, which he remembered for their quiet serenity, looked worried and frightened now.

"Oh, Pete. Are you all right?"

"Hello, Clemi," he said quietly.

He had kissed her not more than twice, he suddenly remembered, and both times had been friendly and casual. He knew she was fond of him, regarding him as Steve's best friend and an indispensable part of the life created here at the Pelican since that day he had come home with Steve after their first Navy hitch. If Clemi felt anything beyond that, she never gave any sign of it, and he had never created an opportunity for intimacy. He wanted to kiss her now, but an awkward restraint fell upon him.

"I was at Kettle Creek," he said. "Where were you, Clemi?"

"Pete, what did they do to you?"

"They beat me up."

She swallowed. He watched the movement of her throat. She made a gesture with her hand as if to touch him.

"Was it Rudge?"

"And Serena Thayer. With two thugs."

"They heard me talking to you last night. They listened on the extension phone. But they didn't let on. Pete, didn't you get my letters?"

"The mail is still in Tokyo. I was shifted to a hospital ship and stayed a while at Pearl before they took me to L.A."

"You said your leg—"

"It's partly metal now. But I get around."

She swallowed again, eyes searching his face. "An accident?"

"Just that. Is it true that Steve sold out to Thayer?" His voice was suddenly harsh, urgent. "Did he sell out, Clemi?"

"You have to understand how it was, Pete. Don't be angry with Steve. So much has happened since you left. And for the last six weeks I've tried so hard to get in touch with you. I didn't know where you were, except that you were with the Navy somewhere in the Pacific . . ."

"I'll tell you about it some other time, Clemi."

"Yes." She clasped her hands before her. "Anyway, Rudge heard me talk to you on the phone. And then this afternoon, as I was about to leave to meet you, he stopped me."

"Rudge is staying at the Pelican?"

"Officially, he's general manager. He stays in Thayer's house on the Point most of the time. Rudge said Alton Thayer wanted to see me in the office. I didn't dare let them know you were coming back. I didn't realize that they had overheard me on the extension line. And Thayer locked the door and talked and talked and wouldn't let me go. When I finally demanded that he let me out of there, he—he made me stay."

"By force?"

She rubbed her arm. "Yes."

He saw the bruises when she took her hand from her arm, and his mouth hardened with a rage deeper than before. It was hot and still in the apartment over the boat-house. From far off came the faint shouts and laughter of some Pelican guests on the tennis courts.

"Pete, don't look like that," she whispered. "He didn't really hurt me. Having Steve in jail is bad enough. I couldn't stand it if anything happened to you, too. It's what Thayer would want, you know. To get rid of both of you. He's changed everything in the Pelican. It's a different clientele, a hard crowd. He knows you won't go along with it. That's why I wanted to see you first, to make sure you don't do anything foolish, like Steve."

Byrum went to the window and looked down at the cove and his boat. A rowboat with an outboard went by the opening of the cove, heading for the hotel anchorage. A man and a woman were in it. Beyond, the sand islands merged with the haze of heat out over the Gulf. The sky looked yellow and unnatural.

He spoke with his back to her. "Sit down, Clemi, and tell me about it. None of it makes sense to me right now."

"Pete?" Light footsteps sounded behind him and he turned. She stood very close to him. Her perfume was light and delicate. Her skin was deeply golden, her lashes delicate fans against her cheek as she looked down at an amethyst ring on her finger. He had given her the ring on her last birthday. She wore no other jewelry except a small, fine pearl necklace that was a Dulaney heirloom. "Pete, please don't be angry with Steve or me."

"He had no right to sell out to Thayer. Thayer represents

organized crime," Byrum said. "It's true we run a gambling joint here, no matter what else you might call it, but it's been a clean, honest place. And we fought off Thayer once when he tried to muscle in. Now he owns half of it. What happened to Steve? Did he lose his mind?"

"In a way," Clemi whispered.

Pete wanted to smash something. Then he looked into her eyes and she raised her hand and touched the bruise on his jaw with cool, gentle fingers. He took her by the shoulders.

"Clemi, how bad is the trouble?"

"As bad as it can be. But don't make it worse, Pete. Please listen to me. Alton Thayer has Sheriff Jergens in his pocket now. Jergens took your money once to keep things quiet when you started the gambling room, but now Thayer has doubled the graft. Are we so much better than Thayer, after all?" She paused, her eyes troubled. "You remember all the nuisances the sheriff inflicted on us when Thayer put the pressure on last year to buy us out."

"We beat him off then. But he's in for good now, thanks to Steve. Why did he do it?"

She looked away. "It's Thayer's wife. Myra Thayer. Do you remember her? He had just married her when you went back into the Navy."

Byrum was startled. "The girl from Atlanta?"

"Steve fell in love with her," Clemi whispered.

He remembered Myra Thayer. She came from an old Georgia family, impoverished and aristocratic. A quiet, dark-haired girl whose social status was one of the things Alton Thayer had hungered for. A pretty girl, young and fine, with a spirit that would be totally crushed by Thayer's brutal strength. Steve and Myra . . .

"I could use a drink," Byrum said.

"I don't understand it completely, myself," Clemi said quietly. "Steve just fell in love with her. She came into the Pelican now and then for dinner, mostly without an escort, sometimes with Thayer or Rudge. Steve didn't want to make an issue of their coming to eat at our place. I know you felt they shouldn't even be allowed on the premises, but once Steve met Myra, he changed."

"And how does she feel about him?"

Clemi's hazel eyes were deeply troubled. "I like her, Pete. I honestly do. She had to marry Alton—her family put so much pressure on her because of Thayer's financial support. He helped her father in business, or something like that. Anyway, it's obvious she married Thayer as a business arrangement. She hates him. She— I honestly think she loves Steve."

"You don't think Thayer put her to work on Steve to soften him up?"

"Maybe that's the way it started. But I don't know."

"When did he sell out his share of the Pelican?"

"A month ago."

Byrum had been on the hospital ship then. "Didn't Steve talk to you about it?"

"No. He was acting strangely for weeks before I learned anything definite. He told me later he—he went gambling in New Orleans. You know how Steve is. It started out in a small way and he fell into a trap. Thayer was behind that, of course. Steve got in deeper and deeper—and just couldn't stop."

"Did he actually get any cash from Thayer?"

"About four thousand for his share of the Pelican," Clemi whispered.

Byrum was shocked. "But his share is worth ten times that."

"I know. But I don't know how much Steve lost in New Orleans. It must have been an enormous amount. And then —two weeks after Thayer moved in—Steve killed that man." Clemi's lips trembled. She picked up an ash tray, put it down, walked to the doorway of the gallery and looked out over the cove and the Gulf.

"Tell me about it, Clemi."

"Steve was like a crazy man. He kept saying how he had betrayed you, sold you out. And what you would do when you came back. He was frantic, trying to figure out a way to make it right with you. And it didn't get better when Thayer and the syndicate began changing everything at the Pelican." Clemi's skirt rustled as she swung around to face Byrum. Her eyes were haunted. "And all the time Steve was mixed up about Myra. He kept seeing her, took chances to see her alone. Finally, Thayer learned about it. He told Steve to get out of town or—be killed."

"What did Steve do around the Pelican after he sold out to Thayer?"

"He kept on managing it for a while, keeping the books, showing Rudge how to run it. Thayer fired most of our staff, Pete. But when the syndicate people showed up, Steve walked out and wouldn't set foot in here again. He went to Maury Harris, and even to Sheriff Jergens, but nothing happened. After that—well, Steve drank and went out on his boat a lot and saw Myra every night he could."

"What about the man Steve is supposed to have killed?"

"Adam Fahey. He was a cheap little detective from New Orleans."

"Rudge told me he was just a waterfront loafer."

"Yes, that's the story for the public. But Fahey was a private detective brought down here by Thayer. He hired Fahey to shadow Steve and Myra. I guess he didn't want to publicize his own humiliation."

"Did Steve really kill this Fahey?"

"He thinks he did."

"Thinks? Doesn't he know?"

"Steve admits he fought with Fahey and knocked him out on the docks that night. Steve had been out in his boat with Myra, and Fahey was waiting on the dock with a camera when they came in. It was late—about two 'clock in the morning. So there were no witnesses. And Myra hasn't said much that can help Steve. Steve tried to take the camera from Fahey; they got into a tangle and Steve hit him and Fahey fell down. He didn't get up again, and they left him there on the dock. Nobody has seen Fahey since, but they found his cap out in the harbor and some of his things—they think Fahey fell off the dock when he was coming to, and drowned."

"That's not first-degree murder," Byrum said.

"That's what Steve is charged with," Clemi whispered.

Byrum was silent. The pattern seemed clear now. Thayer had used his wife to soften up Steve, get him to gamble, into debt over his head, and then moved in to claim Steve's interest in the Pelican. Even then, Steve remained hoodwinked by Myra. Perhaps that part of Thayer's scheme had boomeranged and they were really in love, which would explain Thayer hiring Fahey, the detective, to make sure of his suspicions. But the charge of murder smelled to high heaven. There was no body. There was no proof that Steve was guilty of anything more than having a fight with the man.

He moved about restlessly, noting for the first time how the apartment had been cleaned up for his arrival. There were new monk's cloth curtains at the windows overlooking the Gulf, and a smell of furniture polish on the cypress-and-chintz chairs. Clemi looked defeated, her eyes touching his and then turning away.

"It's not totally bad," he said finally. He stood behind

her and put his hands on her shoulders, and felt her tremble
a little at his touch. He suddenly remembered her as she had
been the first time he saw her, a lanky adolescent kid home
from school for the holidays. She was a woman now. "Clemi,
we can get Maury Harris to help us with Steve."

"I've tried. Maury says he can't do anything."

"If Steve gave up his piece of the Pelican because of
gambling debts, something can be done to challenge the
legality of the deal," Byrum said. "Don't be discouraged.
We can get the Pelican back."

"It isn't just that." She turned helplessly. "The reason I
wanted to see you before you saw anyone—before you saw
Steve—" She paused, bit her ripe lower lip. She was beautiful, and Byrum felt something touch his heart. How had he
been so blind to her before, simply because she was Steve's
kid sister? She said, "Steve has a crazy idea he wants you
to help him with."

"What kind of an idea?"

She said earnestly, "Pete, you don't realize how bad it is.
Something bad will happen—to you as well as to Steve—
if you fight back. That's why I wanted to see you first. I
think you ought to sell out to Thayer now, without any
trouble."

His hands dropped from her shoulders. "No, Clemi."

"But look what they've already done to you, Pete! Beat
you, almost killed you. Steve is in jail. I don't want anything more to happen," she said. "I couldn't stand it."

"Has Thayer frightened you so much?"

"I'm afraid for you. For what they'll do to you."

Byrum touched the welt on his forehead, glimpsed his
bruised face in the mirror. It was an angry and puzzled face.

"Do you want me just to quit?"

"I don't want you to go along with Steve's scheme," she
said.

"Steve's scheme?"

"I told Steve last night that you were coming home. He
was delighted. Up to now, he's dreaded having to face you.
But now he wants you here. He wants you to help him
break out of jail."

Byrum found a crumpled pack of cigarettes and lit one.
He searched her face and found nothing there except deep
concern for him. He said, "Why does Steve think it's necessary to crash out of jail?"

"He feels that Thayer is out to kill him because of Myra.

He says he'll never live to stand trial. Thayer will kill him somehow."

"Then why shouldn't I help him?"

"Because the idea of escape came from Myra, and I suspect it. If he breaks out, it will be an excuse for Jergens to kill him while he's escaping."

"Not if I help," Byrum said.

Something retreated in Clemi's eyes. "Pete, promise me . . ."

"No promises, Clemi. If Steve thinks he's in danger, then we can't take chances, whether Myra is preparing Thayer's trap for him or not."

"Listen," she said fiercely. "Do you think I *like* to ask you to give up? It makes me sick. I hate it. But if you give Thayer what he wants, then Steve will be all right. I'm sure of it."

"Is that what Thayer told you?"

"Not in so many words, but—"

"Then Thayer sent you to talk me into selling out?"

"No, Pete! It isn't like that at all."

Byrum wondered. He had no scruples about helping Steve break out of the Oswanda jail. Considering that Thayer had bought Sheriff Jergens, it wasn't as if he were actually running afoul of the law. Jergens was a fat, mean-eyed man with a greedy palm and a streak of cruelty toward anyone he could bully. No, the law didn't trouble him. It was Clemi, and Steve's affair with Thayer's wife, Myra. Something didn't quite fit the picture there, and he couldn't put his finger on it.

"Clemi, let me look over the Pelican first," he said. "I'll talk to Steve tonight. Make my own decision."

She looked defeated again. "All right, Pete."

"I promise I won't do anything without telling you first."

"All right."

"Clemi?"

She looked up and he suddenly kissed her. Her lips were soft and yielding at first, then her arms came around him and she clung to him with a fierceness that shook him deeply. He felt her tremble against him.

"Help me, Pete," she whispered. "I'm all mixed up. Steve doesn't really know what he's doing. Forgive him for what he did to you . . ."

"It's not a question of that, Clemi."

"You worked so hard. It was your money and drive that got the Pelican started. Steve and I just had the old wreck of a house . . . and now I don't want you to be hurt. I couldn't stand it if Thayer hurt you, too."

He let her go. "I'll see you later tonight," he said gently.

She nodded. "I'm still in the cottage—the one behind the old stables." Her hair shone cleanly in the hot sunlight and there was a glint of fine golden down on her arms. "Please—be very careful."

He looked back through the bathroom door that stood ajar and saw the Colt .38 he had taken from his dresser. It looked bright and dangerous in the sunlight. Clemi followed his gaze but said nothing.

"Are any beachwagons available?" he asked. "My car is up on jacks in the garage. It will need servicing after six months."

"I'll order it done for you."

He watched her go downstairs to the boat dock, moving with the fluid grace innate in everything she did. The sunlight touched her blonde hair and outlined her body in her white sharkskin dress. He hoped she would turn to look back at him, but she walked out of sight along the path to the Inn without turning her head.

Chapter Four

The dining room was busy when Byrum entered. A panoramic window with a long series of French doors opening on the front porch yielded a view of the anchorage, the purpling shore and the glaring surface of the Gulf. A hot wind blew onshore, bringing with it odors of swamp and pines and oil. A few sails bent before the wind in the channel, beating in toward the anchorage. A long causeway curved north toward the barrier shoals a mile offshore, and now and then the sunlight flickered off a speeding car out there.

There were no familiar faces among the dining-room staff. He saw none of the people he and Steve had hired when they had opened for business—loyal people who had stuck with him when payrolls were uncertain and the clientele was practically nonexistent. He felt as if he were a stranger in a place he once had known intimately.

He ordered bourbon at the bar, which was busier than he remembered it, with a loud crowd of patrons in flashy clothes that didn't fit into the serene mood of the old Pelican. He spotted hard-eyed professional girls with too much make-up and bright jewelry. The few elderly couples and quiet young ones who had formerly been the backbone of the Pelican's business looked uncomfortable in the new atmosphere. Byrum ordered pompano from the buxom waitress who served him, and watched the setting sun reflected in a blaze of orange and lavender from the sea.

He did not introduce himself to any of the staff who passed him or waited on him. Spanish John, the bartender he had originally hired, was gone. A man who looked like a thug had replaced him. Music was piped from a recorder somewhere. An orchestra was programed for dancing later in the evening. The new atmosphere grated on his nerves and he pushed his way into the kitchen over the surprised protests of his waitress.

He wore a white dinner jacket and dark slacks and a dark bow tie, and under the jacket was the Colt .38, heavy and reassuring. The kitchen looked changed, the stainless-steel urns and vats not quite so shining and immaculate as they used to be.

"Pete! Pete Byrum!"

It was Albert DeVaux, the Cajun head chef, the first familiar face Byrum had seen. He was a roly-poly man, round face shining with sweat, a powder-white apron and chef's hat atilt on his bald head. He came past the sub-chefs and pounded Byrum's shoulder.

"You are back, *mon ami!* The sailor home from the sea!"

"But not in very good time, Albert," Byrum said. "I see things have changed."

The grin faded from the chef's face. "Yes, is so. But you are well? You have seen Miss Dulaney?"

"Clemi told me what happened. Are you all right, Albert?"

"Only as can be expected." The chef shrugged. "I ask for this and that, I get only half of what is needed. These people—bah, they are short-order cooks, fit for a roadside joint. I quit this Saturday. But maybe now you are back, Pete—"

"Is Thayer around?" Byrum asked.

"Upstairs in his office. You have not talked with him yet?"

"Only with his stooges," Byrum said grimly. "Take it easy, Albert. And don't quit yet."

"If you say not, Pete. If you need help—anything, you understand—you call on me."

Byrum went up the wide, gracious staircase that had been retained from the original design of the old mansion. The ballroom in the front was locked, the double doors securely closed, and a man sat in a plush chair tilted against the paneled wall, reading a comic book. The man wore a dinner jacket that looked uncomfortable on his pug's shoulders. He was sweating, his face small and hard.

"The wheels don't spin until ten o'clock, friend. No admittance until then."

"Where is Thayer?"

The pug jerked a thumb. "Office."

"I'll look at the wheels first," Byrum said.

He had a ring of master keys that fitted every room in the Pelican. He had fitted the proper one into the lock of the white, double-leafed door when the pug came up out of his chair, his face enraged.

"Look, friend, I told you nice to get away from there!"

The man put a hard grip on Byrum's arm. Pete dropped his arm under the other's weight and sank a hard fist into the pug's stomach. The breath went out of the man with a grunt and he doubled forward. Byrum chopped at his neck, caught him and dropped him back into his chair. The pug inhaled with a whistling sound.

"My name is Byrum. Peter Byrum. Watch your tongue next time."

Astonishment glimmered in the pug's glazed eyes. Byrum turned the key and went into the gambling room, snapping on the light switch to his left as he entered.

A low whistle of surprise escaped him. Thayer had spent money with a lavish hand here. Behind him, he heard the pug stumble to his feet and move down the hall. He paid no attention, his glance jumping from the new roulette wheels and gambling tables to the small glittering bar and the plush draperies that shielded the tall windows. A glittering new chandelier hung from the cove ceiling. A new carpet of deep maroon felt soft and yielding underfoot.

"Byrum?"

He turned. Alton Thayer was behind him, with Rudge. Thayer's voice was deep and controlled, and not unfriendly. He smiled from his wheelchair.

"You really should have introduced yourself to the staff," Thayer said. "Johnny apologizes for his rudeness. But you can understand he simply follows orders. This room isn't open until later in the evening. May I be among the first to welcome you home, Byrum?"

Thayer's strong hand was outstretched. Byrum ignored it. His eyes were almost black as he studied the man who represented organized crime throughout this whole territory, this man who was now his partner. Thayer looked big even in his wheelchair, hard and fit and distinguished in a well-cut dinner jacket. A light black blanket covered his legs. In his face was a hardness that made Rudge's handsome brutality look like the twisted emotional illness of a delinquent. Thayer's pale eyes regarded Byrum's tall figure with faint amusement. A large diamond glinted on his finger as he lifted his hand to Rudge, standing beside him.

"Tell the staff that Mr. Byrum is here. We don't want any more misunderstandings, Charley."

"Like the one a couple of hours ago?" Byrum asked.

"I wanted to see you. Obviously, such tactics were unnecessary, since you are here now. It was a mistake. I told Rudge you were not the sort of man to be intimidated. I know how you feel about me and what I represent. But when you examine our books for the last month, your feelings will change for the better."

"How much does the syndicate take?"

"Forty per cent." Thayer smiled, and his face might have been charming except for the bleak gray eyes. "It's insurance, of course, from the law as well as from others who might get ambitious. We hardly tapped you last year—a few broken windows and so forth. It could have been much more serious. The law won't bother us. Our profit margin is going up. People enjoy themselves at the Pelican and exercise their own discretion as to their choice of amusements. We simply give them the opportunity to indulge their particular vices, that's all. But modern times mean modern methods. There's no place for the lone operator today. You get in trouble, it brings trouble to our other places. So we've taken you in. We bought out your lawyer, Maury Harris, and your law, Sheriff Jergens. A wise man takes precautions."

"Like getting Steve Dulaney put away?"

Something moved in Thayer's eyes. "Dulaney is an anachronism in this day. He belongs on a horse, riding his feudal cotton fields. He was doomed to kill himself tilting against windmills."

"With a little push from you."

"Have you seen Steve yet?"

"I intend to tonight."

"Good. Then you will have both sides of the story. You may be more agreeable to my offer to buy you out." Thayer laughed softly. "See? I come directly to the point. I own half of the Pelican now. We want your half, too, and we're willing to be generous. We don't have to be enemies, Byrum."

"We can't be anything else," Byrum said.

"Perhaps seventy thousand dollars will change your mind."

"Is that your offer?"

"We can afford to be generous."

Byrum heard the muted dinner music drifting up from the dining room below, mingled with the clink of glasses in the bar, a burst of laughter from Thayer's hired girls. Too much of himself had gone into the Pelican, too much time and effort and sweat.

"It's not enough," he said.

Rudge said in an ugly voice, "I told you that you can't dicker with him, Al. He won't listen. My way is best."

Thayer sighed. "You and your fists, Charles."

"I could pound some sense into him," Rudge said. He looked at Byrum with hatred. There was that incident of last year when Byrum had thrown him out of the Pelican during Thayer's first abortive attempt to take over. Rudge had waited a long time to get even and he was impatient. "If you leave it to me, Al, I can handle everything for you."

Thayer ignored him and looked thoughtfully at Byrum. "How can I persuade you? More money?"

"No."

"If I arrange matters so Steve is set free?"

"He's not a murderer."

"The law thinks he killed a man," Thayer said.

"Your law. I know you can get Steve out of jail as easily as you put him there."

"Well?"

"No."

Thayer frowned. "You make it difficult for us to work as partners. Neither you nor I control a majority share of the Pelican. How will we make decisions?"

"We don't," Byrum said.

"I've only begun to exploit the Pelican," Thayer said. "I have other plans for this place. And I enjoy being an inn-keeper, oddly enough. I won't tolerate any obstructions from you, Byrum." Thayer paused. "Ten thousand dollars more?"

"You're wasting your time," Byrum said.

He started around Thayer's wheelchair. Rudge made a quick move as if to stop him, and Thayer lifted a hand. "Let him go, Charles. Let him talk to his friends. He'll soon see that it will pay to be reasonable."

"He's just a punk," Rudge said. His amber eyes were dangerous. "I could beat some sense into him."

Thayer sighed again. "I'm sure you could. And Serena would enjoy watching you. But it won't be necessary. Good night, Byrum."

Byrum walked downstairs and out into the open air. The sun was setting and a red glare struck off the sea. He felt the heat like a warm wave rolling over him as he quit the air-conditioned Pelican. His face ached, and his ribs where he had been beaten on his boat. He was conscious of a weariness he hadn't known before that accident on the carrier in the South China Sea.

There were three beachwagons in the garage beyond the tennis courts, keys in all of them. The courts were empty now. He kept thinking of Clemi and of the taste of her mouth when he had kissed her.

He chose the nearest beachwagon with the white pelican on the door panel, and he had the motor started when he heard someone come in through the big doorway behind him.

"Mr. Byrum?"

She had been running to catch him before he left. She was small and delicately boned, with a heart-shaped face and dark hair that fell softly to her shoulders. Her eyes were big, a dark questioning blue.

"Mr. Byrum." She put her hand on the door. "I'm Myra Thayer."

He shut off the motor. She had come here alone and she breathed with difficulty, but her tension was not due to having hurried after him. She looked over her shoulder at the long rolling lawn behind Pelican Lodge. Nobody was here. He watched the rise and fall of her breasts, the quick pulse of a blue vein in her temple.

"Yes, Mrs. Thayer?"

"May I sit with you? I don't want Rudge or Alton to see me here with you."

"Are you all right?"

"Yes. Yes, I suppose so. I'm frightened. I can't seem— I've been frightened for weeks. I suppose it's getting me down."

He opened the door and she slid in. Myra Thayer looked very young and defenseless. Her fragile beauty would have appealed to Steve Dulaney's wild strength, yet her figure was full and feminine. She wore a wide red skirt of iced cotton and a white nylon blouse with a frilly red jabot at her throat. He watched her swallow nervously.

"I can imagine what you think of me, Mr. Byrum—"

"Make it Pete."

"Thank you."

"Are you in love with Steve?"

"Yes," she whispered. "Very much. Did Clemi tell you?"

"Do you plan to divorce Alton Thayer?"

"He won't let me. It's so— There's so much to explain," she said hurriedly. Again she looked back over her shoulder. "I'm worried about Rudge. He doesn't usually let me out of his sight this long. But I don't care."

"What do you want with me?" Byrum asked.

"All I hope is that you'll listen with an open mind. Steve and I couldn't help ourselves. It—just happened, that's all. I never loved Alton. I guess Clemi told you something about that, too."

"Yes, she did."

She tried to smile, but her mouth trembled and she looked down at her fingers, plucking at her skirt. "I suppose I've always been naïve. Sheltered. My family brought me up as if I were—oh, something that needed constant protection. I'd never met a man like Thayer—or Steve, either. I—I was so miserable, I don't know what I'd have done if it hadn't been for Steve. If he hadn't loved me, too."

"Is he a murderer?"

She paled. "Oh, no! You mustn't believe that!"

"Is Thayer going to do more to him, beyond putting him in jail?"

"Yes. That's why I took this chance—to talk to you. To get you to help. I heard Alton talking with Rudge. There isn't much time." She looked up suddenly. "You don't believe me, do you?"

"You want me to help Steve break out of Oswanda's jail?"

"He's got to get out! Tonight!" Her hands were clenched in her lap. He saw the shine of tears in her eyes. "I'm sorry. I'm doing this all wrong. You don't know me and there's no reason you should trust me. I understand how Clemi feels. She isn't sure—she thinks if it wasn't for me nothing would have happened to Steve."

"Take it easy," Byrum said.

She bit her lip and turned away on the seat of the car, her stiff cotton skirt rustling. He gave her the white handkerchief from his breast pocket. She looked as naïve as she sounded. Poor little rich girl, he thought drily, sold to the highest bidder—who happened to be a tough, crippled racketeer operating under a façade of respectability. On the other hand, she could be here now on Thayer's direct orders, working on him to lay a trap that might kill Steve and put Pete Byrum behind bars, too. It could be. But he didn't quite believe that.

Myra Thayer bowed her head. "Excuse me," she whispered. "I don't like making a fool of myself like this. But everything is so mixed up. I'm in love with Steve. You must believe that. And he loves me. I didn't have anything to do with the way Alton got Steve's share of the Pelican. I didn't know anything about it until it was all over and Steve told me how much he had lost in gambling."

"Why was he gambling?"

"He wanted a lot of money, quickly."

"Why?"

"So we could—so we could run away together. I told him it didn't matter, that you would buy him out when you came back. But he said that wasn't fair to you. Every cent he had was tied up in the Pelican and he wanted enough so we could get away from Alton completely without selling any part of the Pelican. So he gambled. And he lost. He lost everything. The Pelican, too, as it turned out."

"Didn't Thayer know about you two?"

"We didn't think so. But I suppose he must have. And I guess he set up that place in New Orleans where Steve gambled. It was crooked—that's why he lost so much. Maybe Alton knew about us and arranged everything to turn out this way."

"But Thayer knows about you now?"

"Yes," she whispered.

"And he wants Steve out of the way for good."

"Yes. Your return has taken him by surprise. He wants action quickly. Tonight he—tonight the sheriff is going to—do something. I don't know what. Steve wants to see you right away."

Myra Thayer's words had a convincing ring, Byrum thought.

"What about this man Fahey that Steve is supposed to have killed?" he asked.

"We don't know. Steve says it could have happened that way. He was following us and he found us on the dock when we came back. He was vile and abusive, and Steve hit him—"

"Didn't you make a statement to the police?"

"Of course. I told Sheriff Jergens exactly what happened. And then Alton came to the jail and he talked to Jergens and the sheriff took my signed statement and put it away and I haven't heard of it since."

"What does Maury Harris think about it?"

"Your lawyer?" She looked down at her hands. "He refused to take the case."

"Maury refused?"

"He's no longer working for you or Steve. He works for Alton. Alton bought him just as he bought everyone in Oswanda." She paused. "Steve will never be brought to trial, because my testimony could get him off with accidental manslaughter, at the most. Alton doesn't want that. He wants revenge on Steve. So if anything happens to Steve tonight, it will be all my fault. But you don't believe me, do you?"

"I haven't made up my mind yet," he said.

She straightened and got out of the car. "If you believe him—and me—then will you meet me later? At ten o'clock, behind the stables here? Near Clemi's place."

He nodded. "Suppose I help Steve get out and it works. What do you expect to do then?"

"Steve and I are going to run away."

"How far do you think you'll get?"

"We have to try. It will work out, I know it will. It must!"

He had the feeling he was talking to a child. Myra obviously had no idea of what she was letting herself in for, running away with a fugitive while she was married to Thayer. The thing was senseless.

She walked away quickly, vanishing in the dusk. He waited until she had entered the Pelican by a side door leading from the yacht anchorage and then he backed the beach-wagon out of the garage and headed toward town.

The Oswanda jail was a one-story structure of cinder block on the courthouse square, just inland from the town landing. It was almost dark when he parked in a diagonal slot on Main Street and got out. Neon lights shone from the poolroom, the bars, the Seacoast Diner, the marquee of Oswanda's movie house, the auto agency. The fading light made the corrugated roofs of the waterfront sheds look like liquid lavender. A few loafers in shirt sleeves and denims lounged against the shed walls and on the benches in the square, where the grass looked beaten to death by the August heat. Mosquitoes whined hungrily under the live oaks as he walked by.

Byrum went into the jailhouse. The front of the building consisted of the sheriff's office, with a storeroom on the left and lavatories on the right. Beyond the two desks, one for the sheriff and one for his first deputy, was a wide corridor to the back of the building, bisecting the cell block, three cells to each side. There was a low wooden rail and a swinging oak gate that barred entry to the rear of the office, but the steel door to the cell rows was open and a dim bulb burned back there, near a skylight in the corridor roof.

Sheriff Jergens was behind his desk. He had been sheriff for nineteen years and had grown fat in office, physically and financially. No one else was in the jailhouse. Jergens wore a khaki uniform with a Sam Browne belt, and directly behind him was a locked gun-rack with four shotguns and two rifles visible through the glass. Great half-moons of dark sweat stained the fat man's shirt under his massive arms. He was totally bald, his skull sunk into the folds of fat around his neck. His neck was of the same dimension as his head so that his skull looked like a simple extension of the column of flesh and muscle rising from his shoulders. He was reading the *Picayune-Times,* and he put the newspaper down carefully on his scarred desk and then put his big hands flat on it, leaning back in the creaky swivel chair that seemed to have taken on the shape of his huge haunches.

"Well, well. Lieutenant Peter Byrum, of the U.S. Navy." He spoke in a thick drawl. "Home from the wars, hey, man?"

"Not a war. Just Reserve training duty."

"Hear you got yourself wounded."

"It was just an accident."

"A hero," Jergens said. "Saved your shipmate, I hear."

Byrum smothered irritation. "I guess you know why I've come straight here."

"Nobody expected you back." Jergens had small, careful eyes. "Didn't come straight here, though. Hung around Kettle Channel for a while, had a little talk with Clemi Dulaney in your place over at the hotel, and had dinner there, too, and another talk with Mr. Thayer. Not straight here."

"You're well informed," Byrum said.

Jergens sighed and reached behind him on the wall for a ring of keys. "Reckon you'd like to see our star boarder, hey?"

"In a moment, Sheriff. I'd like to hear about Steve from you first, if you don't mind. And to get things straight."

Byrum's voice hardened. "You took money from me to look the other way about my gambling equipment at the Pelican. We got along, you and I. Now I guess that's over, Am I right?"

"Don't remember any money from you," Jergens said blandly. "None at all. If I did, it's over, yeah. Right. As for Steve, there's no trouble. It's simple. Your friend got itchy for Thayer's wife . . . got to drinkin' and gamblin' like a crazy fool. Mr. Thayer didn't like it one bit. You blame him?"

"I'm reserving judgment," Byrum said.

"Right. You always were the cool one. Yankee trait, I reckon. How long you been in Oswanda, Byrum?"

"About six years."

"You worked hard at the Pelican."

"Hard enough."

"You aim to let Thayer have the rest of it?"

"No."

Jergens' laughter was sudden and explosive, a high braying noise. His vast belly shook. When he lifted his big hands off the desk, he left sweaty imprints of his palms on the newsprint. The ring of keys jingled as he tossed them across the desk.

"You're a fool, man. But I reckon you don't know any better. Never saw a Yankee yet who could resist an easy dollar, though. Way I hear it, Mr. Thayer made a right decent offer for your share of the Pelican."

Byrum ignored the comment. "You and I had a reasonable arrangement. I suppose Thayer pays you more to shut your eyes to the fact that the syndicate is moving in and taking over your town."

Jergens looked amused. "Poppycock, man. I been over to the Pelican. Never saw anything out of the way to worry about."

"How much does Thayer pay you now?" Byrum asked.

Jergens stood up with a lurch. His saddle nose looked shiny, the small nostrils flaring like an animal catching a dangerous scent. "You be careful, man. Very careful. Hear me? Whatever is in the Pelican, you don't forget it's half yours." Jergens blew out a sudden breath. The air in the jailhouse was hot and breathless, a compound of corn liquor, antiseptic, gun oil and death. A big Colt was holstered in a gun belt that sagged under the sheriff's enormous belly, and sweat darkened the wide seat of Jergens' pants as he kicked back his swivel chair and picked up the jail keys again. "You go on and see Steve. He killed a man. Don't make any mistake about it, Byrum. He's going to be tried for murder."

"You don't have Fahey's body," Byrum said quietly.

"We're lookin' and we'll find it. I got a feelin' we'll come up with it any day now. Your friend Steve killed him, beat him to death because Fahey caught him lovin' up Mr. Thayer's wife on the town landing. Beat him to death with his fists. Go on in and talk to him. I trust you with the keys."

"No, thanks," Byrum said. "You open the door."

"Huh?"

"You keep the keys. Lock me in with him while we talk."

The flush of anger on the sheriff's face slowly faded. He looked amused again. "Smart for a Yankee. Damned smart."

"Let's go," Byrum said.

Chapter Five

Steve Dulaney stood against the far wall of his cell looking out at the narrow glimpse of darkening square and neon lights on Oswanda's dusty, heat-crushed Main Street. It was incredibly hot in the cinder-block jail and the skylight in the outer corridor, designed for ventilation, looked as if it had not been opened since it was installed. Byrum felt sweat start out all over him as Jergens locked the cell door and went away.

Dulaney was tall and lean and fine-boned, with thick yellow hair, long at the nape of his neck. Generations of refinement were revealed in the delicate structure of bone and tissue. He was taller than Byrum, thinner, with long hands that might have belonged to a surgeon or a concert pianist. But there was nothing soft about him. *He belongs to another age,* Byrum thought, *an age of freebooting and buccaneering. He's lost against the syndicate.*

When Steve turned from the window, Byrum was shocked by the change in his face. The blue eyes, so much like Clemi's, were haunted and dark. There were lines around the mouth that had been laughing and reckless, a look of gravity and trouble.

"Pete. You're back! Clemi said you were coming back. I almost didn't believe her!"

They shook hands, an awkwardness between them. A slow grin began and faded on the blond man's face. "You got yourself cut up a bit, Clemi said."

Byrum shrugged. "A flame-out crashed and I went to pull the idiot out and his .50's cut loose from the fire. I took one in the leg and another through the belly. I'm all right now."

"Good. Sit down, Pete." Steve ran shaky fingers through his thick hair. He wet his lips and smiled thinly. "Hell, I don't know what to say to you."

The cell was narrow, lighted by a single naked bulb. There were no other prisoners. That would help if he went along with Myra's plan to get Steve out of here. Byrum surprised himself by even considering it.

"I don't know how to tell you, Pete," Steve said. His voice was strained. "I guess Clemi told you what a fool I was. I guess you think I really ratted and sold you out."

"A fool, yes. A rat, no." Byrum smiled.

"It's Myra," Steve said in a low voice. "You don't know how it's been for her. A nightmare. We're in love, Pete. For the first time, I'm in love, and it's for real."

"Clemi isn't sure about that," Byrum said.

"I know. She thinks maybe Myra takes orders from Thayer. That's hogwash, Pete. She hasn't a dishonest bone in her body. But I didn't play it smart at all. I lost every round. Tried to raise money quick and fell into Thayer's trap. Crooked wheels, maybe, or just too anxious. And I got careless about seeing Myra. How in hell can you ever forgive me, Pete, for doing this to you?"

"It might have happened, anyway. The syndicate's wanted the Pelican for a long time." Byrum lit a cigarette and tossed the pack to the blond man. The jailhouse was quiet. Moths fluttered and danced around the glaring night light. A telephone rang in the front office and went on ringing five times before it was answered. He wondered if the sheriff had been out in the corridor listening. He sighed. "What's done is done. The question is what do we do about it now."

"Have you seen Myra?" Steve asked.

"For a few minutes. She told me what you want to do."

"I've got to get out of here, Pete." Steve turned abruptly, and again Byrum was shocked by the look on his face. Fear was there, something he had never seen in the old days. A fine beading of sweat laced Steve's upper lip. "Thayer is after me, Pete. He's going to kill me. He won't rest easy until the score is even. I've taken his wife from him—and he set a lot of store on his marriage to Myra. He swindled me —thanks to my own stupidity in gambling at one of the syndicate joints—and he got my share of the Pelican. He made me betray you. But most of all, there's Myra. He can't afford to let me live. He framed me on this murder charge—"

"Did you kill Fahey?"

"I don't know. It might have happened the way Jergens says."

"He was unconscious when you left him on the dock?"

"Out cold."

"But he wasn't dead?"

"Oh, no. He was still breathing."

"And Jergens says he must have come to enough to get up and fall off the dock?"

"Maybe. But even if I get charged with simple manslaughter, it'll mean five years in prison. I can't take that, Pete. I can't leave Myra with that sadistic bastard, married to him like that."

"So you want out."

"Thayer isn't sure I'll be convicted. He intends to make sure he's rid of me. Tonight, Myra says. They're going to find me dead here in the morning. Suicide." Steve's voice shook and he dragged at the cigarette Byrum had given him. His eyes slid to the barred door. "I refused dinner tonight. I'm afraid to eat what Jergens gives me. He might put dope in it to make it easier for them."

Byrum looked incredulous. "Steve, this sort of thing just doesn't happen like that."

"It's happening, all right. You can believe Myra." Steve pressed his face against the bars of the door, trying to see down the skylighted corridor to the front office. His knuckles shone white as he gripped the steel. "You didn't come home any too soon, Pete. You're going to help, aren't you?"

"In any way I can. But what you and Myra plan to do—"

"It's the only way. Believe me, Pete. Thayer owns this town. Jergens, everybody. And he bought out Maury Harris."

"Where will you go?"

"Out of the country."

"How long do you think you can last?"

"It will get Myra away from Thayer."

"And what kind of life do you think you'll have, running all the time? Not just from the law either. Thayer will never stop hunting you."

"Pete, don't lecture me." Steve's voice was thin. "We're going. With your help, or without it."

"And if you miss?"

"Nothing to lose."

Byrum said carefully, "You must love her very much, Steve."

"I do."

He was silent. Maybe Steve was right. He drew a deep breath and got up to drop his cigarette into the toilet in the opposite corner of the cell.

"Listen, Steve. This Fahey you think you killed—isn't there a good chance he's still alive?"

"He might be," Dulaney nodded.

"If he is, and we could find him, there won't be any charge against you."

"You'll never find him."

"But if I do?" Byrum insisted.

"In the first place, if Fahey is alive and hiding somewhere pretending to be dead on Thayer's orders, he's a long, long way from here and you haven't a chance of digging him up. There isn't time for it. Thayer wants to get rid of me. Your return now is like a match to a dynamite fuse. He's got to act and act fast. He's jealous about Myra and he's had his way in Oswanda too long to let people go snickering behind his back because of her." Dulaney paced back and forth in the narrow cell. Distantly from a jukebox in the Seashore Café came the thumping rhythm of rock and roll. Voices drifted into the jail from men sitting and talking in the courthouse square. It was totally dark out now. Dulaney said flatly, "Even if you take the time to look for him, Pete, it won't do any good, because by tomorrow I'll either be dead or out of here."

"But Thayer may have been taken by surprise about Fahey, too," Byrum insisted. "He didn't know I was coming back, so maybe he thought he was safe about Fahey and maybe Fahey is still within reach."

Dulaney looked angry. "Damn it, Pete, don't you understand what I'm saying? They're going to kill me tonight!"

"Where did Fahey stay when he was in Oswanda?" Byrum asked.

Dulaney's hands gestured in despair. "That kind of character doesn't take long finding a home. He got himself a woman over in Bugtown and shacked up with her."

"What's her name?"

"Flo Gilligan."

"Where is she now?"

"How would I know?" Steve asked despairingly. "Flo won't tell you anything."

"Maybe she can be persuaded."

Dulaney said, "Chances are she hasn't any idea where he is—*if* he *is* alive."

"If Fahey is alive," Byrum repeated softly. "There's a good chance Thayer will make sure he's dead now."

Dulaney shook his head. "I've done enough to you, Pete. I guess I was crazy even to think about it when Clemi said you were coming back. I can see your point. If you're caught, and involved in my breaking out, then everything is gone for both of us and Thayer wins anyway."

Byrum stood up. "I'm meeting Myra at ten o'clock tonight," he said. "By then, I'll know what to do."

Dulaney didn't get up. He leaned forward, hands clasped on his knees, staring at the rough concrete floor. He nodded slowly. "All right, Pete."

"I'll see you later, then."

"Maybe," Dulaney said quietly.

Byrum rattled the locked cell door and called for the sheriff. The fat man seemed to take a long time returning. Nothing in Jergens' face indicated suspicion. He bobbed his heavy bald head at Dulaney's motionless figure, then grinned at Byrum.

"Things have changed, hey?"

Evening had brought no relief from the sullen heat clamped over the sea and the land. The was a small line outside the movie ticket office to see a Monroe picture and the bars were brightly lighted. Byrum drove west out of the small business district and then turned inland along the shore road, where fine old houses stood behind sheltering walls and immaculate lawns, and followed the Oswanda River farther inland to Bugtown.

Bugtown was a collection of weatherbeaten shacks and taprooms and crumbling wartime housing left over from the rapid expansion of the naval stores plant when the labor force doubled and tripled during those years. Most of the population was Negro, but a few white fishermen lived along the riverbank where their boats were tied up under the shanty windows. The bartender in the first taproom where he stopped for a beer winked and gave him the directions to where Flo Gilligan lived.

He telephoned Clemi from a booth in the back of the bar, using the private number for her personal quarters behind the Pelican. He let the telephone ring for a long time and then tried his own number, uneasiness riding him. The phone in his rooms over the boathouse rang twice and then was snatched up.

"Clemi?"

"Oh, Pete, I was getting worried. Where are you?"

"Bugtown. What are you doing at my place?"

"Waiting for you. I hoped you'd come over for dinner. What are you doing up the river?"

"Looking for Flo Gilligan."

"Oh. That woman Fahey was supposed to—the one he lived with?"

"Yes. Are you all right?"

She sounded breathless. "Yes. Just worried about you. I heard you saw Thayer and turned down his offer. Serena told me about it."

"Have they bothered you?"

"No. But they're worried about you, Pete."

"If I'm lucky, they'll have plenty more to worry about. You stay at my place until I get back."

"All right." She was silent, then: "Pete?"

"I saw Steve," he said. "And Myra."

"What do you think?"

"I'm inclined to believe them," he said. Again she was silent. "I'll be back in an hour."

Flo's place was on the outskirts of Bugtown, close to the swamps that stretched for miles inland, trackless and dangerous, a wasteland of dead cypress, snakes, herons, wildcats and wild pigs. The road was rough and rutted. The lights were shining in Flo Gilligan's shack. Byrum parked under a vast oleander bush and stepped up on the sagging front porch to the door.

Thin roller shades were drawn over the windows. A light snapped off at his knock, then went on again. The bungalow was built on cypress pilings over the swampy riverbank and footsteps echoed hollowly on the pine floor inside. He thought he heard the muttering of a man's voice and then he listened to silence and the shrill scream of an animal in the black brooding swamp behind the house. He touched the solid bulge of the Colt he had taken from the beachwagon and felt reassured.

A car was parked in the shadows beyond the house, a dusty Ford sedan. Light glinted off the windshield. He looked back along the dark lane he had followed from the main highway and saw only shadows. The river made small purling noises. A fish jumped, splashing, faintly phosphorescent. He knocked again.

A woman's high heels tapped to the door. "Who is it?"

"Miss Gilligan?"

"Who is it?"

"Let me in," Byrum said.

"I'm busy. Go on, beat it, you hear?"

He palmed the rusty knob and slammed his shoulder against the flimsy panel. The lock snapped with a sharp metallic sound. The door slapped hard against the woman, who stumbled backward as he shoved in. His glance took in shabby cypress furniture, the sagging pine floor; cheap bright scatter rugs and chintz curtains. Two open doors led back into the rear of the house from the living room, but those rooms were dark. A whiskey bottle was rolling across the floor, gurgling and spilling its contents.

Byrum heeled the door shut behind him.

Flo Gilligan wasn't more than twenty and she might have been stunningly beautiful a year or two ago. There was Indian blood in her, a flush of copper under her prominent cheekbones, a fullness to her lower lip caught between white strong teeth. Her shoulder-length hair was a rich black. Her eyes were venomous as she took in Byrum's dinner clothes. She had lived hard and furiously in her young life, and it showed in the premature lines at the corners of her eyes, in a puffiness along her throat.

"Get out," she whispered. "I don't care who you are. I don't do business like this."

"I just want to talk to you," Byrum said.

"You busted my lock. You can just bust right out, or I'll call the cops."

A small scraping noise came from one of the dark rooms. Byrum picked up the rolling whiskey bottle and set it down on a deal table. It was cheap whiskey. Two glasses were on the table. A man's white straw hat lay on one of the chairs. A photograph was pinned to the pine wall over a record player and Byrum looked at it. It was the face of the small redheaded man who had been on the fishing boat earlier today at Kettle Creek, the one who had been drunk and noisy just before he passed out and was rushed below by his two companions.

He looked at Flo. "My name is Byrum. Peter Byrum."

It meant nothing to her. "So what?"

"I want to talk to you about Adam Fahey."

"You go to hell."

She backed away toward one of the rear doors.

"I just want to help. He's in pretty serious trouble, isn't he?"

"Adam Fahey is dead," she snapped.

"No, he's here. He came here to hide this afternoon, didn't he?"

"Who did you say you are?"

"Peter Byrum. I own part of the Pelican—"

"Then your partner killed Adam," she whispered. Her eyes were narrowed to dark slits of shiny black. "Get out, hear me? Get out!"

"I'll look in that room first," Byrum said.

She was fast. The little ivory-handled fishknife had been strapped to the soft inside of her coppery thigh. She had fought with a knife before. Her left arm went out for balance and she held the blade low, point up, making little circling moves with it as she advanced toward him.

Byrum did not retreat as she crossed the room in slow, stalking steps. The light glinted on the sharp blade, her wet lower lip.

"Don't do anything foolish," he said quietly.

He heard the shrilling of insects in the swamp, the distant hum of a plane over the coast, the slide and scrape of her high-heeled shoes as he watched the knife darting forward like the tongue of a snake. She made a grunting sound and struck, the tip of the knife slicing through his sleeve. He caught her wrist, twisting fast and hard.

"Damn you, damn you. . . ." She writhed in his grasp.

He twisted again, joltingly, and the knife clattered to the floor. He kicked it aside, threw her back from him, stamped on the blade and snapped it. The girl hit the wall and slid to the floor, her eyes blazing.

"Now take it easy," Byrum said.

He started for the back room and there came a slamming of footsteps, the sound of a door being yanked open. He dived through, the Colt .38 in his hand. A man stood outlined against the back door, his body small and taut, crouching. Beyond him was moonlight and shadow on the swamp.

"Fahey!"

The man started to run. Byrum fired one shot over his head, another to his left. The man stumbled and fell face down in the mud. Byrum jumped from the back doorstep and ran toward him. The man struggled up to a sitting position, skittering back on his haunches in the muck as Byrum approached with the gun in his hand.

"Please . . . don't kill me!"

"Fahey?" Byrum asked.

"Yeah . . . You're the guy this afternoon—on the boat . . ."

It was the same man whose appearance on the fishing boat had caused Rudge such consternation. He wore a shabby seersucker suit, dirty sneakers, a striped silk shirt and a black string tie. He was small and wiry and his hair looked red in the light streaming from the back door. His eyes were glazed with terror. He held his hands palm out, as if to push away the sight of Byrum's gun.

"So you're not dead," Byrum said. He felt a vast relief. "Not dead at all."

"Who sent you here? Thayer?"

"Are you expecting him?"

Fahey licked his lips. "Look, don't kill me. I promise you, I promise I'm gettin' out of town now, Flo will give me a lift to Orleans. We was just talkin' about it. I'm buyin' a plane ticket to Caracas. I won't make no trouble, honest!"

Byrum looked back at the house. There was no sign of Flo Gilligan. He shifted position so that he had the dark swamp at his back, facing the shack and the river. The girl did not appear.

"What were you doing on the fishing boat today?" he asked.

"That's where they kept me." Fahey's voice was stronger now. His little eyes, like shiny dark stones, glistened with hope. "You said your name is Byrum, huh?" He drew a shaky breath. "You're the one they heard was comin' back. Gave 'em a hell of a jolt. They wasn't expectin' you, pal. You got 'em runnin' in circles."

"Did Thayer pay you to disappear and pretend to be dead?"

"Yeah, yeah. That was it. But he didn't pay enough."

"You put the bite on him for more money?"

"Yeah, I did that." Fahey nodded jerkily. He swallowed, his Adam's apple moving up and down in his scrawny throat. "Look, it ain't as if I was gonna let Dulaney swing for murder. I'd never let 'em do that. I was just goin' along for the ride, no real harm in it. Thayer wanted Dulaney in jail for a time, is all. No real harm meant."

"I'll bet."

Fahey looked cunning now. "Thayer didn't send you, did he?"

"What do you think?"

"I pretended to be drunk all the time so they'd think I was harmless. After they jumped you this afternoon, I figured I didn't have much time left. Thayer wants me dead—really dead, now. So I snuck off the boat and came here. Flo said she'd take care of me, go with me. But I need some money. I gotta get away from Thayer before he kills me."

Byrum looked down at the man. There was truth in Fahey's words, mingled with cunning and avarice. Fahey was afraid, had been terrified until a moment ago, when he realized that Byrum was not a gunman sent by Thayer to turn a mock murder into reality. He was silent, thinking swiftly how to turn this to his advantage. It had been a stroke of luck to stumble on Fahey like this. Almost too lucky. He gestured with his gun.

"Get up," he said harshly.

Fahey scrunched back. "W-wait. You need me, pal. Dulaney's in jail and they're gonna get rid of him, too."

"How do you know?"

"I heard Rudge talkin' about it. Thayer ain't gonna let Dulaney stay alive after he fooled with his wife."

Fahey's face shone with sweat in the shaft of light from the back door. He wondered if Flo Gilligan were watching from a dark window of the shack.

"Get up," he said again. "Get into the house."

"We can make a deal, Byrum. You need me."

He was worried about the girl. "Flo!"

There was no answer from the shack. Fahey got slowly to his feet, mud slipping from the seat of his seersucker pants. He walked ahead of Byrum back to the house. The shack stood silent and empty. The girl was gone. The front door stood open to the dark, insect-ridden night.

"Do you trust her?" Pete asked Fahey.

"She's my woman. She loves me."

"More than money?"

"Hell, I don't—what do you mean?"

"Thayer might have bought her. She could have been holding you here for Rudge's gun tonight."

"I—I don't believe—" Fear returned to the red-headed man. "Look, I'll give it to you straight, Mr. Byrum. Maybe you know some of it, anyway. Thayer hired me—I got a private office, investigator, see? I do work for the board—you know who I mean? Then Thayer borrowed me to watch his wife. And I did. Dulaney like to've kill me, but he went away before he finished. Then Rudge come along and stuck me on the fishin' boat and told me to stay out of sight. Promised me a grand. I ain't seen five bucks of it yet, though," Fahey finished bitterly.

And now, Byrum thought, Thayer wants to turn pretense into reality. But he did not feel sorry for the frightened man.

"You're coming with me," he said.

"Where to?"

"The jail. Sheriff Jergens. Then we call the newspapers."

Fahey's mouth went agape. He swallowed noisily. "I—I can't do that. They'll kill me there. I'd take the fall myself."

"The newspapers will cover you once it gets into print. They won't dare touch you then. Maybe we can work out a deal for you."

"Thayer would kill me for it!"

"He's going to kill you, anyway."

"But the sheriff— I won't last out the night! You don't know. Jergens is on Thayer's payroll, and Thayer will blow sky-high—"

"Just what I want him to do." Byrum gestured with his gun. "Now move."

Fahey spoke thinly. "Look. Suppose I sign a statement and you give it to the cops and the newspapers and give me a couple hours to catch the plane for Venezuela—"

"No. Move. I want you in person. Alive." He was still worried about the missing girl.

"Give me a break," Fahey whispered. "I'm hit either way."

"You're getting a break. A chance to stay alive. Don't try to run, Fahey. Maybe I won't shoot to kill, but I could put a slug in your knee."

"All right. I'll go along with you," Fahey whispered.

He straightened and turned to walk out on the plank porch that faced the moonlit river.

There was no warning. The shot came from the wall of dark vegetation on the other side of the narrow road. The muzzle flame split the darkness with orange and Byrum heard a chunking sound as the bullet struck Fahey. Fahey screamed and the sound of it rode over the second shot. He stumbled and fell halfway down the wooden steps to the ground. The first shot had ripped through his stomach and smashed his spine. His legs twisted and jerked in spasms. The second shot had gone through his face, smashing teeth and cartilage. His short scream was strangled and inhuman.

Byrum dived from the porch and hit the ground on hands and knees, holding the Colt up out of the mud. There was a boat on the river, a sleek little runabout, moonlight glinting on polished chrome and brass fittings. The dark shapes of a man and a woman rode in it, crouching. He fired twice, got up and ran across the road, hitting dirt again behind the oleander bush. The runabout's motor coughed and suddenly roared, moving out into midstream into a patch of clear moonlight. He saw the man and woman in it quite distinctly.

Rudge. And Flo Gilligan.

His hunch had been right: the place had been designed as a death trap for Fahey. And it had succeeded.

Byrum fired twice more. The runabout's engine raced and a plume of white broke from her bow. A shot from Rudge's gun splattered mud over his shoulder and he ducked. When he looked up, the speedboat was moving fast around the bend in the river. He stood up, braced the Colt on his left arm, aimed at Rudge in the moonlight. He fired, but he could not tell whether his aim was true in the tricky light. The speedboat vanished around the curve in the river, screened by the overhanging moss from the swamp oaks.

Byrum ran back to Adam Fahey.

Fahey's legs were still twitching. There was a pool of dark blood soaking into the earth under his belly. He lay face down, some of his teeth glistening in the dirt a few inches from his head.

"Fahey . . ."

The legs stopped their spasmodic motions. Fahey was dead.

Byrum stood up slowly. The enormity of what had happened began to hit him like a series of shock waves. Fahey was truly dead now. And it didn't matter that Steve would now be freed of the original charge of murder.

Byrum drew a deep, uncertain breath.

With Sheriff Jergens on Thayer's payroll, Byrum's story that Rudge was the killer would be dismissed, never brought to public light. The trap had been perfectly planned, perfectly executed. He was slated to take Steve Dulaney's place in jail. This time, the charge of murder would be backed up by a bullet-shattered corpse.

He looked down at the dead man. Everything Myra Thayer had said was true. Steve would be killed tonight, fixed to look like a morbid suicide in his jail cell. And he, Byrum, would then take Steve's place. With Jergens in charge, the frame would be easy.

Byrum turned and began to run.

Chapter Six

He reached the beachwagon and with his hand on the car door forced himself to stop and breathe deeply. The river flowed like smooth black silk through the salt marshes toward the Gulf. A bird called eerily in the darkness. There was no sign of the speedboat now; the sound of the motor was gone. And this made suspicion suddenly flare above the hammering of his heart. Maybe Rudge had decided to come back, to end the job by finishing him along with Adam Fahey. He was alone for the moment but not for long.

He swallowed air, then turned and trudged back toward the shack that stood on stilts above the mud of the riverbank. Weeds rustled and crackled as he cut across the abandoned lawn.

Byrum went inside the shack, turned on the porch light and looked at the small redheaded man crumpled on the sagging porch steps.

Get rid of the body, he thought. *Hide it.*

He was sweating when he reached down and grabbed Fahey by one arm, lifting him from the floor. Instantly he felt the pull and strain on the scars in his stomach; but he couldn't quit. The night was hot and still, filled with rank odors from the river and the swamp. Fahey was surprisingly heavy for his size. There was a small puddle of blood and shredded flesh on the porch under his head. Nothing could be done about that. He hoisted the dead man to his shoulder, again feeling the thrust on his stomach scars.

On the second step down from the creaking porch—without warning—the rotted plank suddenly yielded with a groan of punky wood. The dead man on his shoulder, Byrum felt his leg twist and wrench under him as he fell. One of the boards swung up and slammed into his side. Pain seared through his body and leg like a white-hot flame. Grunting, Byrum pushed himself upright in the muddy soil and rolled the dead man's weight off him.

For several moments he waited for the pain to ebb. The porch steps had collapsed completely on one end. He pushed a plank off his leg and tried to stand. His knees felt like rubber. Waves of nausea moved up from the scars he carried. He tried a step or two, limping badly, but he could walk. He looked down at the dead man. Short of dragging Fahey fifty yards through the mud and brush to where his car was parked, he didn't see how he could move the body at all.

Byrum pushed himself back up to the front door and snapped off the porch light. And then he heard the distant wail of a siren.

The sound came from downriver, moving toward Bugtown, coming fast. Rudge hadn't wasted any time in getting to Sheriff Jergens.

There was no chance of dragging Fahey's body to the beachwagon. The siren grew louder and nearer as he listened. The acute pain in his stomach ebbed, leaving only a pulsing ache there. The shack stood silent and dark on its cypress stilts, four feet above ground level at one end and a foot or so at the back end where the land lifted with the slope of the riverbank. Weeds and brush had grown up around the openings and underneath, beyond the weedy vegetation, was a yawning area of dark secrecy.

It might work, Byrum thought. The obvious might never occur to Jergens. Not immediately, anyway.

The siren was growing steadily louder. Grunting, he began to push and heave at the dead man, rolling him under the house into the dark, careless of the brambles and the mud. Fahey's body was obstinate, as if possessed of a stubborn determination to balk him. Five feet in. Ten. Byrum paused, panting and sweating in the stifling darkness under the house. Something scuttled away from him toward the rear where the timbers came down close to the damp, sucking soil. A rock loomed like a dark obstacle a few yards farther in. He drew a deep breath and resumed the struggle, cramming Fahey's body behind the sunken boulder so that a casual flashlight beam, if shone in from the porch, would not pick up his position.

It was done. Not more than three minutes had passed, but Byrum was shaking with fatigue. Headlights flickered on the rutted road at the bend of the river. He got up and ran, limping, toward the beachwagon.

The lane did not end at Flo Gilligan's place. It looped away from the river, circling past another deserted cabin with the roof fallen in, and then rejoined the road heading back toward Bugtown. Byrum drove without lights. Twenty feet from where the ruts rejoined the lane, he stopped the car in the brush, the motor idling. He saw the headlights intermittently through the swamp and then the full glare of the beams probed through the green foliage, sweeping over him and going by.

It was Sheriff Jergens. Byrum glimpsed the police insigne on the white door of the sedan. The police car went by toward Flo Gilligan's shack and he eased into gear and drove the bouncing beachwagon onto the road in the opposite direction.

The neon lights of the taproom in Bugtown where he had stopped to inquire about Flo Gilligan's place shone through the black night, and Byrum pulled the beachwagon into the graveled parking lot behind three other cars and cut the motor. He shrugged out of his stained and torn dinner jacket and thrust it under a piece of canvas in the back of the car. He left the .38 Colt in the car. Then he pulled off his necktie and rolled up the sleeves of his shirt and opened his collar. His trousers were mudstained. The ache in his abdomen was almost gone.

The jukebox was thumping and the same fishermen were still in their places, sweaty and red-eyed. Nobody looked at him twice. He headed for the telephone booth in the rear and dialed Clemi's private number.

The phone rang. He sweated. The phone rang once more.

"Hello?"

"This is Pete," he said quickly. "Are you alone?"

"Yes. What is it? You sound—"

"It's trouble. Lots of it. I found Adam Fahey."

"Oh, no . . ."

"He was alive when I found him, but he's dead now. Rudge shot him. At least I'm pretty sure it was Rudge. The sheriff is looking for me right now."

He heard her draw a deep, shaken breath and then listened to a humming silence. The jukebox shook the pine floor of the bar. A woman had entered from the parking-lot door and stood with her back to him at the far end of the bar, laughing up at a big fisherman in a red sports shirt and white cotton trousers with a fishknife thrust into his wide leather belt.

"Clemi?"

She sounded breathless. "What can I do, Pete?"

A wave of relief went over him. He said, "I'm supposed to meet Myra at ten o'clock in the old stables. She was going to tell me her plans for Steve. Do you know what they are?"

"No."

"Then you'll have to get her. Don't let anybody see you talking to her. Understand?"

"I'll meet Myra. And then?"

"Bring her with you. Use your car. If nobody sees you leave the Pelican, so much the better. I don't want you involved, Clemi."

"I'm already involved," she said. "With Steve—and with you."

He paused, aware of the other meaning of her words. "All right. Bring some half-inch manila line, about thirty feet, off my boat. And a small grappling hook and a crowbar. You'll find most of the stuff in the bow compartment. Take a couple of flashlights, too. And I need a change of clothes. In my apartment there's a black sweater and some dark slacks. I'll need a pair of sneakers. Find the blue ones. Nothing white to show in the dark. Got that?"

"Yes, Pete."

"Are you all right, Clemi?"

"Yes. Where shall we meet?"

"On Barney Ti-Bo's wharf, the far end. It's right across from the jail." Sweat dripped down his face and soaked his shirt. He couldn't breathe in the phone booth. "Get there before ten. As soon as you can."

"All right, Pete. Be careful."

"Good girl, Clemi."

She had hung up. He pushed open the booth doors, went over to the bar and ordered bourbon. The bartender's eyes lingered for a moment longer than necessary on his face before he put the shot glass on the wet zinc bar and poured. Byrum rested his weight on his right hip, favoring his strained muscles.

The woman at the far end of the bar turned and stared straight at him.

It was Serena Thayer.

She wore a plum-colored cotton print dress with a yellow cashmere sweater over her narrow shoulders. Her red hair was tied in a short pony-tail that was too youthful for her face, swinging and jerking with the nervous twitch of her head. Her pale cat's eyes, too big for her narrow face, widened as she recognized Byrum and smiled. She had on too much lipstick, as usual, and she waved a filmy handkerchief in one hand, saying something to the big fisherman, who scowled, and then she came walking over to Byrum.

"Petey, darling! What on earth are you going here?"

He met her wide stare blandly. "Drinking," he said. "What about you?"

"Well, heavens, I had a date and here I am. Do you know George? He owns the *Maryjane*, a shrimp boat. He's a friend of Brother's."

"No, I don't know George," Byrum said. "Good-bye, Serena."

"But, darling, you're not angry at *me* for what Rudge did—"

The fisherman came up along the bar like a tug pushing at a barge against the tide. His voice rumbled. "Let the punk go, baby. You and me—"

Serena giggled. "George, Petey doesn't think you're good enough to be introduced to him."

The fisherman glowered, not understanding. "Yeah?"

"Drop it in the bucket," Byrum said. His mind raced, assessing the meaning of Serena's presence here. Did she know about Adam Fahey? She could have been in the run-about with Rudge and the Gilligan girl. Her eyes looked strange. Queer little highlights pinwheeled behind her popping stare. Her bony face was shiny under the heavy make-up and her lipstick was smeared at one corner. She flipped the perfumed handkerchief she clutched in her hand.

"Maybe Petey doesn't think I'm good enough to talk to, either," she pouted. "He thinks Brother and I are just trash. Why, heavens, I just throw myself at this man all the time, George, and he treats me like—like I was another Flo Gilligan."

She knows, Byrum thought. He looked at her wide, laughing mouth, at her garish lipstick, and something cold ran up his spine. She had been with Rudge in the boat.

The fisherman looked confused. He knew he was being forced into an argument with Byrum, but there was a bovine placidity in him that resisted quick action.

"You apologize to the lady," George rumbled.

"What for?"

"For what you said to her."

"Good," Serena said. "Show him, George. Make him apologize."

Byrum stood on the edge of danger. George was flattered by Serena's attention, puffed up by having a date with Al Thayer's sister. He wondered if Serena had been posted here at the bar to look for him. No, they couldn't have expected him to escape from Flo Gilligan's shack. They had figured him for a dead pigeon, fluttering into Sheriff Jergens' fat arms. He looked at the way she touched the tip of her tongue to her lips.

"All right," he said. "I apologize."

"Really, Petey? What for?" she asked.

"For thinking of you as I do," he said. He couldn't help himself. "For considering you a perverted tramp."

"Hey," George said.

Byrum hit him with a chopping left, threw the bourbon in his face as George reeled against the bar, and hit him again in the stomach. The big man went down, groping for the fishknife in his belt. When he got it in his hand, Byrum kicked it away. He felt Serena claw at his back, screaming something, and he swung and hit her squarely on her open mouth. Her eyes popped open, stunned. He caught her as she fell, an angular dead weight in his arms, a parody of a woman. He lowered her to a chair and she fell forward over the table. George was out cold, the victim of a glass jaw. An abrupt silence fell over the bar.

There were three other men, two girls, and the bartender in the place, rooted by surprise. Then one of the girls screamed. Byrum plunged for the door and the darkness of the night.

He had the beachwagon started before they came yelling out of the bar entrance. He backed wildly and one of the men yelped and dodged out of the way. He swung in a hard, screaming circle out of the parking lot and hit the concrete at sixty miles an hour. There was nothing ahead but the lights of Oswanda beyond the causeway to Bugtown. Nobody in the bar had followed him.

Barney Ti-Bo's wharf was beyond the courthouse square, to the left of Oswanda's town landing. It thrust out into the small harbor between other wharves, dark and smelly, the heat of the day still radiating from the corrugated tin sheds built flush with the stringpiece on one side. The tires of the car rumbled hollowly on the planks as Byrum drove to the far end of the pier and halted in the deep darkness beyond the shed. The wharf building sheltered him from the lights of the town landing and the square beyond. When he cut the engine and sat back dragging deeply at a cigarette, he heard the slap of the tide, the creak and groan of hawsers on the half-dozen shrimp boats tied rocking to the stringpiece. The moon was gone, but starshine glimmered on the harbor water, making long crystalline ribbons of blue ice on the Gulf farther out beyond the light buoy. The air was dead and motionless; it tasted of brass. The temperature was in the nineties.

He picked the gun up from the car seat and slid the action back, caught the cartridge that popped out and clipped it into the bottom of the magazine. What would Thayer do now?

For a moment he gave way to anger against Steve Dulaney, against Steve's wild temperament. Of all the women to fall in love with, Steve had had to fall for Thayer's new wife.

But since when had love ever made sense? You've known Clemi for over six years, Byrum thought, and she was just a nice kid hanging around during the summer months and holidays. And except for the times when she argued against the wheels you'd installed in the Pelican, you never really looked at her or thought about her until you thought you might die in that naval hospital in Tokyo. And when Dr. Stein pulled you out of it, you suddenly couldn't wait to see her again. And all at once you looked at her and really saw her this afternoon, and she was a woman, lovely and altogether desirable. You saw what she felt for you in her eyes and you knew without a word being said that she had loved you for a long, long time, while you had hurt her, through ignorance, by accepting her presence so casually and without thought.

Byrum shook his head in the darkness and dragged at the cigarette. The thing to do now was to stop Thayer. Thayer worked on two drives—his lust for power, his plan to take over the Lodge. That was cold and calculated, a finely planned business maneuver. The other business with Steve was because of Myra, and in this, Thayer was plunging ahead on raw, primitive instinct. A man like Thayer could never tolerate the knowledge that the man who had taken his wife from him was still alive.

Steve was right. Myra was right. Thayer would never let Steve see the dawn come up through his cell window. Not after Adam Fahey's death tonight, not after wrapping a quick frame around Byrum to be rid of opposition in the Pelican Lodge.

He waited for the two women.

Occasionally he heard the sound of canned music from the bars on Main Street, the drift of voices from the hot, hollow black cave of the courthouse square. A boat moved out into the harbor, engine pulsing over the oily water, lights glimmering red and green in thin ribbons over the blackness. The gun shone softly on the seat beside him.

Clemi and Myra arrived on foot. They had parked in the square, in the dark shadows under the oaks, and they came walking out on Ti-Bo's wharf quickly and silently. The clock in the courthouse tower was ringing ten in the stifling night when Clemi appeared around the corner of the shed.

"Pete?"

"Here," he said. "Did you bring everything?"

"Yes. What happened to you, Pete?"

"I ran into Serena. It's all right now."

Myra was pale. "She's a terrible person. So utterly vicious, you can't imagine—"

"I can imagine. Look the other way, huh? I'm going to change my clothes."

The two women stared out at the harbor as Byrum slipped from the car and took the dark slacks, sneakers and thin sweater Clemi had brought him. He changed swiftly, wadding his muddied shoes and trousers into the back of the beachwagon with his bloody dinner jacket. Clemi wore dark slacks that hugged her long thighs, a wide belt that accentuated her narrow waist, and a dark silk blouse. Her long golden hair was tied in a bun at the nape of her neck. Myra wore a dark skirt that rustled when she moved and a blouse of a slightly lighter shade than Clemi's. She looked small and delicate and nervous. Byrum put the flashlights, grapnel, rope and crowbar together in the beachwagon with his gun.

"All right," he said. "Myra, tell us how you planned to get Steve out of jail."

Her face was dim in the shadows. Her voice was a tight whisper. "Steve worked it out. He'll be ready and waiting for us. You know how the jail is laid out? There's the big front office where Jergens has his desk and guns, and there's the locked steel door to the cells in the back. Just the six cells."

Byrum nodded.

"Well, there's no other way in except the front door, and that's open to the square and anybody could see us going in and out. There are a lot of people sitting on the benches out there under the trees, trying to get a breath of air. But there's a small back door on an alley behind the Seashore Café. Steve said nobody ever uses it. It's always locked and barred. Jergens has the key to it on that ring he hooks on the wall behind his desk."

Byrum nodded again. "Jergens is going to be busy tonight, looking for me."

"That may help," Myra said. "Maybe only a deputy will be on duty." She drew an uncertain breath. "Steve thinks they'll drug his food, so he hasn't eaten any dinner tonight." She watched Byrum nod. "The idea is for me to go in there to see him on the excuse that I'm bringing him a sandwich and coffee, and get Sheriff Jergens, or the deputy on duty, to let me inside the cell block. Then Steve will overpower the deputy while—" She broke off as Byrum shook his head abruptly.

"No good," he said. "They won't let you past the office door tonight."

"But we've got to get in there—"

"The keys are the thing," Byrum said. "We've got to have them. I doubt if we could open that back door, anyway. It probably hasn't been opened since the jailhouse was built." He frowned. "But there's a skylight in the roof over the cell block corridor."

"Yes, I remember that."

"That's the best way. You can keep Jergens busy while I drop down into the corridor behind him and get into the office from that direction."

Clemi said doubtfully, "You'll still be barred from the office and the keys by the door behind Jergens' desk. That's locked, too."

"That part of it will be up to you. About the keys, I mean," Byrum said. "It will have to be timed just right. Can you go through with it without giving it away?"

"Yes," Myra said.

He looked at her for a long moment. This girl was not quite as soft and helpless as she appeared. There was steel in her slim, fragile body. He glanced at Clemi. She was holding herself tightly, her face a dim mask in the shadows, eyes luminous, watching him.

"Myra," he said quietly, "what will you and Steve do, if and when we're successful?"

"We're going to run away."

"Where, exactly?"

"I don't know. Steve said he would let Clemi know where we go."

"Didn't he tell you any more of his plans?"

"No. We just want to—be together."

"What about money?"

Myra said quietly, "I have some. It's my own. I took it from the house before I came here. I have two packed bags in my car, too. Steve and I will be fine once we get out of Oswanda."

Byrum had the feeling she was holding something back. "You know what you're letting yourself in for?" he asked harshly. "The law will hunt for you, and so will Thayer. Thayer will never give up."

"We'll only have to hide for a little time," Myra said.

"When we've proved that Steve is innocent of anything to do with Fahey, we can return."

"Come back here to Thayer's territory?"

"Steve will be able to handle him then."

Clemi said, "But what about you, Pete? They'll know you helped get Steve out."

"They're hunting me now for murder," Byrum said. "It couldn't be any worse."

Chapter Seven

The alley behind the Oswanda jailhouse was a smothering slot of darkness, fetid with smells. The beat of twist music came from the front of the Seashore Café, and from the kitchen in the rear came a clattering of pots and pans and the sizzling crackle of food frying in fat and all the smells and contamination of rot in the still heat of the night.

The alley was not wide. Byrum could touch the back wall of the jailhouse and the back of the café if he extended his arms. The back door of the café allowed a slab of yellow light to fall into the alley on the cinder-block wall of the jail. There were no windows in this wall of the jailhouse, only the solid steel of the back door to the cell block. Byrum stood with the rope in one hand, the light grappling hook bent to one end of the line. He felt the weight of the gun, flashlight and crowbar in his pockets, and for a brief moment he had a feeling of total unreality, wondering why he was here and what he was doing. Then Clemi came walking silently on rubber-soled saddleshoes into the smelly alley and he wished suddenly and fervently that she wasn't in this thing at all.

"Myra got the car parked," she whispered. "It's hers, you know. The Cadillac."

"Did you talk to Steve?"

"I stood under his cell window to light a cigarette. He knows we're coming. He's waiting."

"Did anybody see you?"

"There were some young couples on the park benches, but they were too busy with each other to notice me. It's such a hot night. Pete?"

"Don't worry about it now, Clemi."

"What will happen to you and me?"

"We'll do what we can. We'll get out of it."

"Pete, I waited so long—for you to come back. It was like six years, not six months. I waited for you before that, too, but you didn't know about that. You never knew anything about it, did you? And this time—this time I thought you would look at me and finally—see me. And you did, didn't you?"

"Yes, Clemi."

"But I didn't dream all this would happen, too."

He felt her shudder in the heat. "It will be fine, Clemi. You'll see."

"Steve just went crazy. Myra did it—"

"Do you think she's responsible for this?"

"No, no. She loves Steve. I guess she really does, to risk what she's doing now. She has no illusions about what Thayer will do when he learns she's run off with Steve. But where does that leave you, Pete? It isn't fair to leave you here to face all the trouble."

"I'm different from Steve," he said. "Go back to the car now, Clemi. Send Myra in the front door. Did you see if anybody was in the front office?"

"Jergens just drove up a minute ago. And a deputy."

"Two of them. That's not so good."

"No, there's just Jergens, I think. The deputy drove away."

Clemi started to turn aside, then swung back and touched his arm. Her lips brushed his cheek fleetingly and, without another word, she was gone, moving silently down the alley toward the courthouse square. Byrum waited, counting the seconds.

There came another rattling of pots and pans from the café kitchen. Byrum swung the light grapnel and let it fly up into the darkness above the back wall of the jail. It landed with a thump behind the narrow coping and grated against the crushed-stone roofing before it hooked behind the coping. He stood still, holding the line taut, waiting and listening.

Nothing happened.

Quickly, he hauled himself up hand over hand, his feet in sneakers braced against the cinder-block wall. In a matter of seconds he was up and over, lying prone on the roof fifteen feet above the alley. Again he waited. There was no alarm. He drew a deep breath and stood up, searching the skylight. The heavy rectangle of glass gleamed faintly in the starshine. From the roof he could see the trees in the courthouse square in front of the jail and the lights of the movie marquee two blocks down Main Street.

Kneeling he pried at the skylight with his fingers, then with the bar. He could hear no sound from inside the building below him. Heat lightning shimmered on the horizon of the Gulf. The heavy skylight frame did not yield. He heaved again on the small steel bar, controlling the strength of his effort to avoid any sudden lurch and noise. His probing fingers found no lock here on the outside. He tried again. This time the hatch squealed faintly, yielding an inch or two. It was heavier than he had supposed. He lifted again and this time he brought the skylight up and away from the molding with a faint rusty sound he could not avoid. He slid it to one side.

Light gleamed up through the opening. He looked down onto the concrete floor of the cell block corridor. Nobody was in sight. He returned to the back wall of the jailhouse, retrieved the grapnel and line and hooked the prongs to the frame of the skylight and dropped the line down into the corridor. A moment later he slid inside.

Voices came to him from the front office. Myra was talking to Sheriff Jergens. He heard the pleading urgency in her words.

"Pete?"

The whisper came from Steve's cell, thirty feet back from the barred door to the front office. He saw Steve's hands gripping the bars and then Steve's lean, taut face pressed close to the door. Byrum went silently back to him. Steve's face was pale, a muscle cording along the ridge of his jaw. His whisper was almost soundless.

"Is that Myra?"

"Yes. Take it easy, Steve."

"Thanks. Thanks, Pete."

"You're not out yet."

Byrum turned and slid along the wall toward the barred door to the front office. He could hear Myra Thayer speaking plainly now. The front door to the building stood open and beyond was the square, with people sitting there in plain sight. He frowned. He hadn't thought much about that.

The sheriff's back was toward him. The fat man leaned forward in his cushioned swivel chair, great streaks of sweat darkening his khaki shirt. Myra stood on the other side of the desk, facing the locked door that separated Byrum from the cell keys. The ring of keys, he remembered, was hanging on the wall just a few feet to his right under the case of guns.

Jergens' voice was an irritated rumble. "Look, Mrs.

Thayer, you can't see Dulaney. He's sick. He's been actin'
mighty queer all day, you want the truth about it. Anyway,
you ain't very smart comin' in here like this, when everybody in town knows how Mr. Thayer feels about it."

"I want to see Steve," she insisted thinly. "Right now.
You have no right to hold him. He didn't kill anybody.
Adam Fahey was killed only tonight, and Steve was right here
in jail all the time. You haven't got any kind of a case
against him now."

Jergens' meaty shoulders hunched forward. "So you
know about Fahey, hey? Did Pete Byrum call you?"

"Yes, he did," Myra said defiantly.

"Did you see him?"

"No."

"Mrs. Thayer, I'm going to call your husband on this.
Do you know where Byrum is?"

"Yes, I do. Perhaps, if you let Steve go—"

"I'm busy," Jergens said. "Your husband will come and
take you home."

Byrum wondered if there was anyone else in the front
office. There could be a deputy sitting out of sight, listening. But he heard no other voice or sound. Myra looked
beyond Jergens and saw him, flat against the corridor wall beyond the bars that separated them. Nothing changed in
her small, smooth face. Only contempt showed in her eyes
as she returned her gaze to Jergens. Byrum saw the rolls of
fat on the big man's neck fold and refold as Jergens shook
his head.

"We got an alarm out for Byrum. We're going to get him
and we're going to hang him. Flo Gilligan witnessed the killing. You better co-operate with me, Mrs. Thayer, and forget about seein' Steve tonight. I can't let you in and I ain't
going to let him out without a court order."

"Did you tell him he's to go free? Did you tell him
about Fahey?"

"Not yet, Mrs. Thayer. I been busy. Tomorrow, first
thing, I'll talk to the district attorney about lettin' him out."

"You're lying," she said flatly. "You'll never let him out."

Jergens sounded mildly surprised. "Now what makes you
say that, Mrs. Thayer?"

"You're going to kill him," she said. "I know all about
it."

The fat man's hands came down on the desk with a flat
sound. A flush of red spread over his huge neck and bald
scalp. "Now look here, Mrs. Thayer, I don't tolerate talk

like that even from you. I don't know where you and Dulaney got the crazy notion that something was gonna happen to him here in my jail, but as long as I'm sheriff in Oswanda—"

The telephone rang.

The fat man puffed out a big breath and Byrum watched him reach for the phone. Myra turned away, hands clasped before her, as if to pace nervously back and forth. She came around the desk while Jergens grunted monosyllables into the phone. "Yeah, yeah . . . Serena saw him, hey? . . . Yeah, Bugtown . . . But dammit, he could be anywhere by now—"

The keys jingled suddenly as Myra snatched them from the wall and thrust them through the bars into Byrum's outstretched hand. Jergens suddenly twisted in his swivel chair. He saw Byrum. His jaw dropped in total astonishment. And then he saw Byrum's gun.

"Put down the telephone, Sheriff," Byrum whispered softly. "Do it carefully. Say goodbye to the man. And then don't move, not if you want to live."

Jergens was incredulous. "I been lookin' for you, Yankee boy. And all the time you been in my jail? How—"

"The telephone, Sheriff."

Jergens cradled the phone with care.

Byrum said sharply, "Open the door, Myra."

Jergens said in a thin voice, "What do you think you're doing? How did you get in there?"

"We're taking Steve Dulaney with us."

"Hell, are you crazy?"

The door swung open. Myra slipped past Byrum and ran down the corridor to Steve's cell. Byrum said dangerously, "Don't make any careless moves now, Sheriff. Unless you want your belly to leak."

"You wouldn't shoot me, boy."

"Don't try me. Get in here."

"Steve is gonna be let out tomorrow. Now we know about Fahey, that is."

"You're lying. Thayer wants Steve dead. And you're Thayer's boy for the job."

Jergens' fat face was like pale stone. "You believe that?"

"You framed him and now you're willing to frame me. You know Rudge killed Fahey. But you're not the law here. You're just another one of Thayer's punks. Now get in here, quick."

Jergens pushed heavily through the doorway and stood

across the inner corridor from Byrum. Byrum slapped the heavy cell-block door shut. It locked automatically. There had been no alarm from the street outside. Jergens mopped sweat from his face with a big handkerchief. Byrum slipped the .38 revolver from the sheriff's holster and pocketed it. Jergens grunted angrily and walked with a heavy tread down the cell corridor after Myra, his fat haunches waddling.

"Where did you put Fahey's body, Byrum?" he asked suddenly. "You still got it in your car?"

"I thought you knew all about it," Byrum said.

"We got Flo Gilligan. She'll be a state's witness and we're keepin' her safe. She says you got into a mighty hot argument with Fahey over Dulaney bein' in jail while Fahey was supposed to be dead. She says Fahey tried to run and you shot him. Lost your head, hey?"

"You'll need Fahey's body to prove it," Byrum said.

"We'll find him this time," Jergens said. "Don't be a fool now, Byrum. Use your brains. You're in trouble enough as it is."

"Open Steve's door, Myra," Byrum said.

Steve Dulaney came out of his cell with a rush. His teeth gleamed as he grinned and hugged Myra, then bobbed his head at Byrum. "You did it, friend. I'll never be able to thank you enough." The grin faded as he looked at the sheriff's huge bulk in the stark light of the jail corridor. "You fat scum, I ought to—"

"There isn't time," Byrum cut in. "Get up that rope and onto the roof. Myra, go out the front way to your car. You know where we'll meet?" He watched Myra nod, and said briskly, "All right, Steve. Up on the roof."

There was a reckless look in Steve's eyes as he stared at Sheriff Jergens. He looked as if he wanted to kill the fat man. Byrum grabbed his arm and shoved him toward the rope dangling from the skylight. "Go ahead, Steve. We haven't got all night. Get up that rope!"

Steve tore his wild gaze from the sheriff and went to the dangling line and hoisted himself hand over hand up through the skylight without another word. Byrum looked for Myra. She had already gone through the front door. He swung his gun at the sheriff. "Into the cell, Jergens."

The fat man sweated heavily. "You know what you're doing? They'll laugh at me—locked up in my own jail. And Thayer will kill me."

"That's your lookout. Maybe the Attorney General will

make something out of it. I'm getting him down here to-morrow to clean up this mess," Byrum said flatly. "Now get inside."

Jergens lunged at him, instead. Byrum chopped hard at the fat man, the blow aimed at the side of Jergens' huge throat. He had to hit him twice before the sheriff sagged and went down on his knees, head rolling. Byrum pushed and shoved him into Steve's cell, slammed the door and tossed the keys toward the end of the hallway, then grabbed at the rope. In a moment he was back up on the roof.

Steve was not in sight. Then he saw him, up in plain view of the eave overlooking the courthouse square. Byrum unhooked the grapnel from the skylight coping and walked toward him.

"Steve, what do you think you're doing?"

Dulaney grinned. His eyes were bright. "I just signaled to Myra. She started the car."

They returned toward the alley and in a moment dropped into the fetid darkness behind the Seashore Café. There was no way to get the grapnel loose from the edge of the roof now and Byrum had to abandon it.

"Come on."

They went to the mouth of the alley and stood on the deserted sidewalk around the corner from the square. Steve was drawing in great breaths of the hot night air. Off on the seaward horizon, heat lightning flickered and ribboned against piling masses of great clouds. Music came to them from the bar down the street. In the darkness of the park, a girl giggled and a man talked softly and earnestly.

"Gee, it's great to be out, Petey. You're an ace."

"We're not out of it yet. There's a long road ahead."

"You'll travel it with us, Petey."

"No," Byrum said.

Steve looked at him, his eyes white in the darkness. "But you can't stay here any more than I. To hell with the Pelican. Let Thayer have it. Myra and I will find some other place to start living again."

"The Pelican is ours. I plan to keep it if I can."

"Against Thayer? With a murder rap hanging over you?"

"I'll work out something." Byrum wanted to get Steve off his hands and safely away. There was a nervous quality about him, a bursting pressure that seemed ready to explode into unpredictable violence. "Where is Myra?"

Her car slid around the corner at that moment, parking lights glowing. Steve snatched the door open and jumped in beside her. Byrum remained on the dark sidewalk. There was still no alarm from the jail.

"Get in, get in, Petey," Steve called.

"Where is Clemi?" he asked Myra.

"She went back for the beachwagon."

Byrum swore softly. "All right, go ahead. I'll get Clemi. We'll meet on my boat and decide what to do next."

Steve laughed. "It's all decided, Petey-o."

"We'll talk about it," Byrum said. He slammed the door shut. "Get going."

He watched the heavy car purr away down the narrow street and around the first corner. Uneasiness roweled him. Everything had gone smoothly, yet he wondered in which direction he was plunging.

Nobody interfered with him as he crossed the courthouse square to the waterfront. At Barney Ti-Bo's wharf he paused, searching the darkness for Clemi. There was still no alarm from the jail, yet he felt as if dark shapes were sliding through the night at his heels. It was only the beginning, he thought, of how it felt to be a hunted man.

He stepped onto the wharf planking and heard the beachwagon motor start. Then the car came toward him, materializing out of the lighter darkness of the harbor and the Gulf. Lightning shimmered again to the south and this time he heard the faraway rumble of thunder. The air felt electric, breathless. He waved and saw Clemi behind the wheel. She stopped for him and he jumped in.

"What took you so long?"

He could not see her face clearly in the darkness. "I lost my keys," she said. "Or else Myra stole them. I had to jump the ignition wires. Did you get Steve out all right?"

"What do you mean, Myra stole your keys?"

"Please. Is Steve all right?"

"He's gone with Myra. Answer me, Clemi."

Her voice shook. "We're in trouble, Pete. Steve and Myra have done an awful thing."

"What are you talking about?"

"Myra had a small suitcase in her car. She dropped it by accident while we were waiting and the lock snapped open. I saw what was inside."

Byrum fumbled for a cigarette. "Start driving, Clemi. To my place."

"But won't they look for us there?"

"We're meeting Steve and Myra on my boat. What was inside Myra's suitcase?"

"Money, money, money," Clemi said.

"How much?"

"I couldn't tell. It was hard to guess. Packs of twenties, fifties. Maybe a hundred thousand dollars. Maybe more."

"Whose money? Did Myra say?"

"Alton Thayer's, Pete. She took it from Thayer's house safe. Thayer's collections come in every week—Rudge is the collector from all the horse parlors and joints Thayer runs besides the Pelican—and Thayer keeps the cash in his house because of taxes and records. Twice a month, Rudge takes the syndicate's share to New Orleans. He was due to go tomorrow. But Myra took all that cash. It's their stake, she says. I told her it wouldn't work, but she insisted that she and Steve knew what they were doing."

Byrum gave a soundless whistle of dismay. "I see."

"So I think Myra stole my keys to delay us. They don't intend to meet us, Pete."

"I think they will." Suddenly he grinned at her and leaned over and kissed her cheek. She smelled of fresh soap and perfume. He touched her hand. "It will be all right, Clemi."

"Don't you understand?" she said angrily. "Steve is my brother, but what he's done to you is just terrible. Thayer will go after you, too. Don't you see?"

"I see, all right. We'll talk it over with Steve."

"Pete." Her voice trembled. "It's Thayer's money! It's gangsters' money. And now, with Steve running off with Thayer's wife—"

"Drive, Clemi," he said.

He lit a cigarette. They were going down the main street of Oswanda now. Two men were running toward the jail. The cashier of the movie house, a frizzy-haired blonde, had stepped out of her booth and was staring that way, too.

Chapter Eight

It was going to rain. The offshore wind brought a smell of oil and salt from out of the blackness of the Gulf of Mexico. The wind was hot, like the blast from an open furnace, and the channel beyond the Pelican Lodge anchorage was streaked with dimly visible whitecaps as the first gusts of the approaching storm hit the land.

Byrum told Clemi to drive in by the back road. The lights of Pelican Lodge and the anchorage shone fitfully through the thrashing trees as the wind struck. The back road was only a rutted lane that turned off from the concrete drive circling in toward the main building and the guest cottages on the beach. Byrum glimpsed a number of cars in the parking lot and then a rise of land cut off his view of the main grounds and he saw the old boathouse where he lived.

His voice was quiet. "What else did Myra tell you about their plans, Clemi?"

"They're going to Mexico," Clemi said.

"Are they flying? Or what?"

"They're using Thayer's boat. Insult to injury, I guess. Myra knows how to run it. It's the big one, the fifty-footer. Thayer named it after her when they were married—I believe he gave it to her as a gift. It's called the *Myra T.*, of course."

"Where are they headed for in Mexico?"

"A small fishing town near Vera Cruz. Guayamas."

"Did you know about this before?"

"No, Pete . . . What are we going to do?"

"We'll help them," Byrum said.

"With Thayer's money?"

"No. We'll take that, turn it over to the Attorney General."

"Steve won't give it back. He figures Thayer owes it to him."

"And Myra, too?" Byrum asked acidly.

Clemi's face was pale above the wheel. She turned the car deftly in behind the boathouse and turned off the motor. The wind made thin thrashing sounds in the trees behind them and the *Firefly* nudged the pier with erratic thumping sounds as the bumpers struck the stringpiece. Everything was dark, the stars gone behind the swiftly piling overcast.

"I don't blame you if you're angry with Steve," Clemi whispered. "I could—well, I'm just sick about it. What he's done to you, I mean. None of it is really your fault, Pete, except—well, you made the Pelican into a gambling place yourself. Surely you expected trouble that way."

"I've handled trouble before."

"I know. I know the way it was with you, long ago. Steve told me the little you ever told him. But it was the wrong road to take, Pete. Surely you can see that now. I'm not blaming you. I'm with you, whatever you do. But if we could only get out of this, I wish—I wish you'd go into something else, something better."

Byrum looked around in the shadows. "They're not here."

He got out of the car and felt the push and thrust of the wind, heard the rumble of thunder, much nearer now. "You may have been right. They may not come here at all. But I can't believe it of Steve."

Clemi stood beside him. "I want you to know—whatever you decide to do, it's all right with me."

"You don't have to choose between me and your brother," Byrum said. "I'm not a plaster saint, and I don't know what I'll be in the future. I'm not asking you for any kind of a decision, Clemi."

"I've already made it. Steve couldn't have gotten out of jail without your help, no matter what Myra might have tried. They'd have killed Steve tonight if you hadn't saved him. You don't owe him anything more."

The pressure of the wind whipped her clothing tight against her lovely body. When lightning ribboned across the black sky, he saw the way her hair was blown across her cheek, saw the anxiety in her soft eyes, the way her figure was molded by the thrust of the turbulent air. Turning abruptly, he walked down to the dock and looked at the dim shape of the *Firefly,* lifting and falling restlessly against the restraint of her mooring lines. Clemi followed him to the rocking float.

Nobody was on the boat. He went aboard, came ashore again. Clemi had not moved. She stood facing the hot wind that blew from the empty blackness of the Gulf.

"Pete, they want you for murder now."

"I didn't kill anybody," he said.

"And Thayer has the Pelican. All of it. The Pelican and Jergens and the whole town."

Byrum said grimly, "He doesn't have his wife. And the syndicate's cash. He's not in such a good spot himself, right now. And he doesn't have a pipeline to the Attorney General."

"But if you go there, Pete, you'll have to admit you ran the Pelican as a gambling place."

"Yes."

"What will they do to you?"

"I don't know."

"It will mean the end of everything you worked for."

"Maybe." He looked soberly at her. "It might also be a beginning, a new one. For us, Clemi." He paused, thinking that now was not the time to talk of how he felt. "We'll wait another few minutes. Then I'm going to Maury Harris."

"Your attorney? He won't help. He keeps the books for Thayer now."

"He'll help."

"But suppose Thayer owns him?"

"Suppose the world is made of green cheese, Clemi? The rats would all have a holiday. Stop worrying, please."

"I can't help it. I'm frightened for you."

He kissed her. Her mouth trembled softly against his. Her arms held him, clinging, on the uncertain, rocking float.

"They're not coming," he said. "Let's go. We'll see Maury."

It began to rain.

Clemi said bitterly, "Steve had no right to do this. He promised to meet us. My own brother—"

"Come on," he said.

The rain came down harder.

Maury Harris came to the door himself. The attorney wore a silk bathrobe of bright yellow, and yellow leather slippers. His home was a small bungalow on the Knoll, the residential section of Oswanda back in the pine woods. It was one of half a hundred identical houses built within the past two years and it looked new and raw. Maury Harris didn't look quite so new. In his thirties, with thin black hair, a small mustache meant to be jaunty, and a figure running to fat and a little potbelly, he looked worried and harassed, his dark-circled eyes wide with alarm as he saw Byrum at the door.

"For God's sake," he said. "From bad to worse."

Byrum stood in the rain on the concrete front steps. "Aren't you going to ask me in, Maury?"

"Pete, you've got the whole town on its ear!"

"You make me sick," Byrum said, and pushed past the lawyer into the house. Maury Harris started to pluck at his sleeve and then stopped and peered out into the rain-swept street. Clemi was waiting in the beachwagon with the parking lights on and the motor running.

"Don't wake up Anne and the kids, Pete," Maury said. "Please. They're upset enough as it is."

Byrum's hair was dark and glistening wet. His sweater looked black, plastered to his shoulders and chest. He moved carefully into the living room and yanked the draperies closed over the picture window that looked out into the street. A cut-glass decanter stood on an open bar and he found a glass and poured himself some bourbon. Maury stood watching him with worried eyes. Maury didn't look his sharp, prosperous, and alert self tonight. He looked scared and running. He needed a shave and his thin hair made him look older than his thirties. He had a tic in his left eye.

"Pete, what do you want with me?" he asked.

"I want help."

"Look, your retainer ran out long ago. I don't work for you any more."

"Then for who? Thayer?" Byrum asked sharply.

"I take my clients as they come," Maury said.

"As the syndicate orders you, you mean."

"I don't front for the combine," Maury said quickly. "You know that. The business between you and me was strictly simple stuff, setting up the Lodge, paying off who ever demanded ice—Jergens and his deputies—the mayor— you know. You ran a clean place even if it was outside the law, and we had no trouble."

"So everything was fine and you took a thousand a month from me out of the till. Now we have trouble, Maury, and you fall apart at the seams."

"You know Thayer," Maury whispered. "You know what he'd do to me."

Byrum looked around the room. It was furnished as if everything in it had been taken straight out of a department-store window. He listened, but all he heard was the drumming of torrential rain outside. Maury's wife was upstairs asleep, with Maury's two children. Harris was trying to light a cigarette, but his hand shook too much and the lighter wouldn't work. Byrum crossed the room and caught his hand and steadied it as Maury flicked the wheel and lit up.

"Thanks. I'm a little nervous."

"You're green," Byrum said.

"Thayer is looking for you," Maury said. "So is Jergens. What kind of a stunt did you think you could pull in this town? Busting into jail, taking Steve out. And as for Dulaney—bad enough he stole Thayer's woman. He took all that money, too—"

Byrum took hold of the lapels of Harris' silk robe. "How did you know about that so fast, Maury?"

"Thayer called me. He wanted to know if I'd seen you."

"He told you about the money?"

"He was raving about it. I never heard him like that before. He'll kill Steve on sight. You, too."

"I doubt that." Byrum released the chubby little lawyer. He was sorry he had displayed the flash of temper. Maury looked white and shaken. "Thayer wants Myra back more than the money. What else did he ask of you?"

"If you came here, I was to call him. Right away."

"He wants to see me?"

"Hell, he wants to kill you, Pete."

"And will you call him?"

Maury Harris didn't answer. He didn't have to. Byrum read the reply on his round, slack face. Byrum said, "Did you hear about Fahey, too?"

"Yes."

"Think I cooled him?"

"I don't know what to think."

"At least you know that Steve didn't do it."

"That's right."

"Maury, you could call the state capitol. Tell somebody there how Jergens is owned by Thayer. Tell them about Fahey, about conditions in this town since Thayer took over. You know people there. Maybe Masterson, or John O'Keefe."

"No, no."

"Nothing, Maury?"

"You'd better just run, Pete," Maury said. "I'm sorry."

Byrum could see the telephone through the arched entrance to the hallway. He knew that Harris would call Thayer the moment he stepped out of the door into the rain again. He didn't blame Harris too much. Self-preservation was too strong an instinct to combat with words or pleas or references to honor. His sodden sneakers had left a wet trail across the gray broadloom carpet that covered Maury's living room from wall to wall. The gun in his back pocket sagged heavily.

"I need some money to run, Maury," he said.

"I've only got a hundred or so in the house."

"I'll take it," Byrum said.

Maury Harris went to his desk, pulled out a manila envelope and dumped a thin sheaf of bills on the desktop. Byrum picked it up and stuffed it into his pocket without counting it. "I'll pay you back," he said. "But I want more. Try your safe, Maury."

"The safe?" Maury whispered.

"Where you keep the Pelican's books."

"Now, look, Pete—"

"I want the books, too," Byrum said. "Thayer's books. I'm sending them to John O'Keefe."

"Pete, for God's sake, you'll ruin us all!" Maury whispered. His face was blanched. His hands shook. "Give me a break, Pete. I can't let you take them."

Byrum took out his gun. Harris stared at it. Byrum said, "Alton Thayer wasn't prepared for my homecoming. Otherwise, he'd have yanked his books out of this house. He knows you're a weak sister, Maury, and he wouldn't have trusted you with them. Open the safe, Maury."

Harris moved like a man in a trance toward the opposite wall, pulled aside a framed lithograph that acted as a door hiding the safe dials behind it. He licked his lips.

' "Thayer will kill me. We'll all go down the drain. You're not exactly innocent, either, Pete."

"I'll be happy to take whatever fall the court gives me."

Harris stared at him. "You're ready to dump everything?"

"I have no choice." Byrum thought of Clemi. "Maybe I should have cleaned this up myself, long ago."

"You must be nuts."

"The books, Maury," Byrum urged softly.

The safe came open. There were three ledgers. Byrum tucked them under his arm and walked toward the front door. Maury Harris stood where he was, his eyes the eyes of a dead man.

"You can call Thayer any time," Byrum said.

Chapter Nine

Byrum closed the door softly behind him. The street was deserted in the driving rain except for a few lighted windows toward the corner. Through the wide picture window of Maury Harris' living room he saw the stout little attorney sitting exactly where he had left him, unmoving, his eyes staring at nothing at all. The beachwagon was parked diagonally across the street in the deep shadow of a tree, but he could not make out Clemi's figure behind the wheel in the darkness.

Shielding the ledgers under his arm against the rain, Byrum ran across the wet street toward the waiting car.

Another car was parked farther down the rainswept street and he had not noticed it from the steps of Maury's house. It had not been there before. He saw Clemi's pale face turned toward him from the dimness behind the wheel as he reached for the door to get in, then there was a flicker of dark movement from behind the tree on the sidewalk and the looming bulk of a man sliding swiftly behind him.

"Don't make a move, Byrum."

It was Rudge. Byrum was handicapped by the bulky ledgers clasped under his arm, and taken by total surprise, Rudge had a gun jammed into his back in the next instant.

The big man chuckled. "Al Thayer figured you might make a try for little Maury. I got here just in time to see you go in." His clipped Oxford accent was more pronounced than ever. He slid Byrum's gun free of his back pocket with a sound of satisfaction. "I wouldn't try anything foolish now. Your girl friend is being sensible about it. You do that, too."

Byrum spoke above the hiss of the rain in the street. "What do you want?"

"The books you took from little Maury. That's first. Jergens said you made a crack about going to the Attorney General. I don't think your yarn would be accepted without these records, would it?"

"All right," Byrum said. "Score one for you."

"Next, where did you put Fahey's body?"

"You killed him, didn't you?"

"I won't argue with you about that. But where is he?"

"You'll have to find him yourself," Byrum said.

Rudge had moved around so that Byrum could see his hard, handsome face in the dim illumination from the nearest house windows. The man's pale eyes were cold, speculative. He seemed unaware of the rain that drenched them as they stood beside the car. For a moment, a glittering urge toward violence shone in the man's stare and Byrum braced himself inwardly against the threat of Rudge's gun. Then the moment passed and the man's face grew smooth and bland again.

"You won't be stubborn for long, Petey. Thayer wants to see you. So get in the car and let the girl drive. We'll go there now."

"And if I don't?"

"I wouldn't mind killing you right here."

He meant it. Byrum got into the car, squeezing over next to Clemi so that her thigh was pressed tightly against his. Her voice was low, measured in anguish.

"I couldn't help it, Pete. He took me by surprise. He said he would kill you as you crossed the street if I cried out to warn you."

"It's all right."

"I'm sorry, Pete."

Rudge said, "Let's go. Thayer is anxious. He's biting nails tonight."

He took the ledgers from Byrum's hand.

Alton Thayer pushed his wheelchair away from the window

that overlooked the sea. Black rain pelted against the glass and the raging gusts of wind found an echo of anger in his big frame. His heavy face showed nothing of the frustration in him, however. He would have given anything tonight, anything at all, to be able to walk again. He wanted to be in a dozen places at once—the Lodge, with Jergens, out with the men Rudge had sent to hunt them down. But he was chained to his chair, tied forever to this thing of steel and wood because of one split second of rending metal and overturning, flaming car that had left him with this broken back and only half a man's body.

Serena stood beside the small fire in the fireplace of the study, and Thayer looked at her with cold, dispassionate eyes. She was his sister and he detested her, knowing the destructive drive that ruled her every action. Some built and others tore down. Serena, out of malice or envy or a perverted twist, was one of those who enjoyed destruction.

She was smiling. Her mouth was too wide, with too much lipstick, and her pale eyes were too big and crazily excited, he thought.

"I couldn't hold Byrum at Ozzie's," she said. "I tried, but he got away."

"Did you have to be there at all?" Thayer asked.

"I had a date. Anyway, I wanted to be near."

"How did Fahey die? Did you see it? Did it amuse you?"

"Al, I don't like that sort of talk." She moved her thin hands in the air. "Are we in so very much trouble?"

"Maybe the worst." He sounded grim. With one shove of his powerful shoulders, he pushed his wheelchair to a halt before the table with the liquor decanters on it. The big house was quiet. He had bought this place to look respectable, to do business like a gentleman instead of a hoodlum. Everything was done quietly and properly. It had been going along real fine, he thought bitterly. The alky runs were all set up and he certainly knew how to handle that end of it—most of the runners from the old days were long dead, in prison, or simply vanished. He was one of the few survivors of that school. The Pelican had been pouring money into the till. And now Pete Byrum had to come back and stir up this mess. Killing, now. New Orleans wouldn't like the business of Fahey at all. But what was a man to do? One thing led to another, one kill meant another kill, and how could you stop it now? The pot was boiling and you had to keep the lid clamped down tight. Or else.

Or else you're through, Thayer thought coldly.

Serena was saying, "I want to watch Byrum when you get him, Al. I despise that man."

"I'll bet you do, baby. But we'll have to hump ourselves to catch him. He's quick. And dangerous."

The telephone rang on the big desk and Serena moved to answer it, her heels clacking sharply on the stone floor. This Spanish villa was a mausoleum of stone and depressing mahogany furniture. Thayer watched Serena at the phone, impatiently waiting for whatever message she listened to. He thought of how Rudge had bungled this afternoon, letting Byrum glimpse Fahey on the fishing boat. Rudge was too busy with ambitions of his own.

His mind twisted to Myra, and a quick spurt of anger went through him. Myra, his money, the boat—all gone. He had to find them. To hell with Rudge and the board. He had to show them he could handle anything, legs or no legs. He knew the board was watching him closely on this. And he had to deliver. He had to prove he was still Al Thayer, the boss, on top all the way.

Serena put down the phone and looked at him, her narrow face cruel and arrogant. "That was Maury Harris, Al. Byrum was there. He took some money—and the books."

Thayer felt a stab of fear. "The ledgers?"

"Maury couldn't stop him. I guess Rudge didn't get there in time."

Thayer felt as if a door had been slammed in his face. Fury boiled in him. He heard Serena laugh and he wanted to slap the smirk off her wide, vivid mouth. He did not understand what Byrum was doing and he was afraid of anything he could not understand.

He wondered why Rudge had failed to intercept Byrum. Had Rudge let this happen deliberately? In the back of his mind he saw the man's slow brown eyes watching him. There was contempt in the gunman's stare. But no, that couldn't be. Rudge was tied to him, forever and ever. Or could the board be thinking—no, Rudge didn't have the brains to run this operation. But maybe Rudge knew what the board was thinking—maybe he knew the name of his successor, already on his way to clean up this mess.

Thayer slammed a big hand down on the arm of his chair. It was over an hour since Jergens had called about the jailbreak. Almost at the same time he had found the safe open, the money gone. Myra had taken it. He thought of her cool, disinterested face, the hatred in her eyes; hating him but belonging to him. She was gone now, with another man. Gone with his money and his boat.

He looked up. Serena was watching him over a cigarette. "There's no word on the *Myra* yet," she said. "It's a wild night out on the Gulf. None of our boats are out, Al, are they?"

"No. And nobody saw them leave, either."

"The dock is empty." Serena shrugged. "Maybe Steve and Myra will drown out there, Al. It's a rough night." She frowned and asked suddenly, "Rudge can't swim, can he?"

"No."

"And he doesn't like the water, does he?"

"What's that got to do with it?" Thayer wanted to shout, but he was pleased at the measure of control in his voice. Serena was baiting him for some obscure reason of her own. She actually enjoyed this trouble, waiting with bright-eyed expectancy for his destruction.

And it could happen. Thayer wheeled his chair angrily back to the window. Rain beat heavily against the glass, obscuring what little he could see of the angry night. He wondered if he ought to call New Orleans. But what could he tell them? Rudge had probably already reported the missing money to those men at the conference table. They would want the money back. Fast. No excuses. You produced—or you were eliminated. Fear moved in him with the thought, and then a murderous rage shook him and he looked down at the blanket over his legs. From the waist up, he was the equal of any man. If he could only walk—

He pushed the thought down. Somewhere out there on the storm-tossed Gulf was the answer to all his problems. Out there was his boat, his wife, Steve Dulaney, and his money. They were running now, but they could never run far enough or fast enough or long enough.

Serena divined his thoughts. "Where do you think they're heading, Al?"

"I don't know. It doesn't matter. I'll find them."

"But all that money, Al! What will you tell New Orleans?"

"Shut up!"

"Maybe Byrum knows where they went."

"Maybe." Thayer looked at his sister and wondered at the bright emptiness of her eyes. Serena studied him as if he were some queer insect to be killed and dissected.

She said, "But Byrum is tough, darling. He isn't like Dulaney. He knows how to play this game. If he knows where Steve is, he won't tell you."

"Rudge can make him talk."

"I doubt it." She moistened her lips. "But Charles can make Clemi Dulaney talk." She smiled as Thayer's big, shaggy head jerked up. "Byrum is in love with Clemi. Work on her a little, Al." She giggled. "Let Byrum watch Rudge work on her and he'll probably talk quite fast."

"Yes," Thayer said, nodding. "We'll do that. When we get them."

"Rudge will get them," Serena said. "He has to. What else can he do to prove he's a better man than you?"

Rudge dried his fingertips on his thighs with a meticulous gesture and shook a cigarette from his pack and lit it. There was blood on his knuckles, but he ignored it; it was not his own blood; it came from Byrum.

It was almost midnight. He had called New Orleans twice so far, promising results. Thayer hadn't spoken to the board as yet. Rudge put this down to fear, nothing more. Thayer was finished. He couldn't handle this, with his ideas of keeping things quiet. There were times when force was needed, and that was Rudge's job.

"Well, Byrum?" he asked quietly.

"To hell with you," Byrum said.

It was hard for Byrum to speak. His mouth was bleeding and there were several loose teeth in his jaw. He ached all over. He was in no condition, after his six weeks in the hospital, to take this sort of brutal, efficient battering. There was a numbness all through him. He tried to remember how long it had been since Rudge had forced him into Thayer's house at the point of his gun. An hour? Perhaps a little more. The storm coming in from the Gulf was as wild as before. The wind was close to sixty knots now, coming in lengthening gusts. He didn't think Steve Dulaney was a good enough seaman to survive. Yet for Steve there had been no choice but to run, to risk death by drowning, foundering in Thayer's boat, or face a more certain death here from Rudge.

"Where are they?" Rudge asked. "Where, Byrum?"

"I don't know."

"Where is the money, Byrum?"

"I don't know."

Rudge hit him again, slamming his head back against the wall. There was nothing Byrum could do about it. His hands were tied behind his back. Rudge turned away, dragging at his cigarette, and he had a moment's reprieve. His blurred vision cleared and he saw the room distinctly now.

He was in the servants' quarters of the big, Spanish-type house Thayer lived in, a small room scantily furnished, with a row of casement windows streaming with the rain that battered the south wall of this wing. Rudge leaned against the bare plaster wall looking at him with pale, thoughtful eyes. Serena Thayer sat in a chair opposite, her narrow hands gripping the arms in excitement. Clemi sat stiffly in a chair beside her, looking at nothing at all. Her blond hair was curled and gleaming with the rain that had drenched her. Her eyes were tormented by the pain Byrum held within himself.

Thayer in his wheelchair filled the doorway to the room. His heavy face was flushed and angry and worried. Half an hour had gone by since Rudge had returned with these two. Rudge acted as if his orders were of no importance now, as if he, Rudge, were in command of this thing. The dark fear in Thayer's mind flickered higher now.

Serena spoke from her armchair. "Al, darling, surely you know by now that you're wasting valuable time. Every minute Byrum keeps silent means that Myra and your money are moving farther and farther away. I told you what to do, sweetie. Don't bother with Byrum. Ask Clemi."

Rudge flicked his pale eyes at her and then at Clemi. "I think she's right."

"I don't like to hurt the girl," Thayer said heavily.

"Since when did you get so finicky, darling?" Serena asked.

"Watch your mouth," Thayer snapped.

"Serena is right. You've lost your grip. You got any idea how New Orleans feels about it?"

Thayer said dangerously, "Don't reach too far too fast, Charley. You still take orders from me."

"Ask the girl, Charles," Serena urged. "Go on, ask her."

"Sure," Rudge decided. "We're wasting time."

Clemi had not stirred. She did not look at Byrum, on the floor with his shoulders braced against the wall. She seemed afraid to look at him. Byrum felt a deep twist of horror for her. It didn't matter what they did to him, but if Rudge put his hands on Clemi—

He strained for the tenth time against the ropes that tied his wrists. He looked up and saw Serena smiling at him, enjoying his misery. He wondered what kind of perverted charge she got out of this sort of thing. He looked into her eyes and saw only a spinning emptiness.

Rudge crossed the room and, without warning, slapped Clemi hard across the face. Clemi's head fell back and her long hair swept across her cheek. A small sound escaped her. Thayer sat in his wheelchair and watched.

"Where did Steve and Myra go?" Rudge asked.

"I won't tell you," she whispered.

"You know what I can do to you, baby? You got any idea?"

"I don't care."

"But you know where they went, don't you?"

"No."

"How come you didn't go with them?"

"They didn't want us," she said.

He hit her again and again. Byrum shouted in helpless rage. Nobody looked at him now. Clemi's mouth was bleeding. Serena's quick, impassioned breath made a hissing sound. Rudge lifted his hand again, and Byrum lurched to his feet with an effort and lunged at Rudge's huge figure. His head caught the killer in the stomach and Rudge was knocked backward, the breath grunting out of him. He came back, chopping at Byrum's throat, and Byrum fell to the floor at Serena's feet, hitting the carpet with his shoulder, feeling the wrench at his scarred stomach muscles as he fell. Rudge kicked him and then ignored him. Through a haze, Byrum saw the big man reach for Clemi, twist her hair in his hand and drag her violently from the chair. Her face was a pale mask of defiance. And suddenly Byrum knew that nothing Rudge could possibly do to her would make her divulge Steve's destination. And there were too many things Rudge could do to her. A great wave of defeat moved over him, dark and deep and bitter.

"Wait," he whispered. "Let her go."

Serena said, "Go on, Charles. Work on her."

Byrum said, "Don't hurt her any more." He heard Clemi whisper something, telling him it didn't matter. He alone knew how much it mattered.

"Let her go," he said. "I mean, let her go all the way. I want her to walk out of here."

"I won't go without you, Pete," Clemi whispered.

Rudge said, "Where is Dulaney and the money?"

"Will you let her go?"

"I'll lay off, that's all."

"All right." Byrum knew it was the best he could do. "Steve is heading for a small town on the Mexican coast. Guayamas. You can't overtake them now. Not in this weather."

Rudge laughed. He looked at Thayer's eyes and then he stopped laughing.

Clemi wept.

Otherwise, there was silence in the barren little room. Then Thayer said flatly, "We'll go after them."

"We could fly tomorrow morning," Rudge said. "Be there ready and waiting for them."

"No." Thayer looked at the big man. "Byrum has a big enough boat, we'll use it. We'll go after them that way."

"Are you crazy?" Rudge said angrily. "In this weather, by boat?"

"You're coming, too. I don't need anybody else to help me. Byrum can run the boat. We take his girl along to make sure he doesn't step out of line. And you'll be my legs and gun for me, Rudge."

"No deal," Rudge said. "I don't like it."

"I know. You're afraid, aren't you?"

"Listen, I—chasing them by boat doesn't make sense!"

"Then run back to New Orleans. I'll get another gun. Guns are cheap. I've got plenty of them in this town."

The challenge was final. Rudge's face showed that he understood everything Thayer had left unsaid. The crisis between the two men was close to a climax now. Rudge looked away first, spoke slowly.

"We could fly over there with Johnny Gee and Matt. Nothing to it. Be there waiting for them in the morning. If we chase them in a boat, we might never catch up." His voice hardened. "You're putting it all on me, Thayer. I'll have to watch Byrum and the girl, do all the rough work. You'll be worse than useless in that chair."

Thayer's heavy face was dark. "Then stay here. Serena and I will handle it."

"You're taking a chance with the syndicate's money. You know what happens if you lose?"

"You're wasting time," Thayer rasped. "You know what happens if I go to New Orleans and get aboard a plane? People know me. There'd be newspaper photos. There'd be questions asked. Everything we did from then on would be watched. We couldn't touch Dulaney. And you're not going there alone. So we go by boat. Quietly. With nobody paying attention and nobody knowing what happens when we catch up with them."

"At least," Rudge urged, "let's leave Byrum and the Dulaney girl here. We can turn 'em over to Jergens."

"No. I'll need them."

"You think they'll help?" Rudge jeered.

"They'll have to," Thayer said. His heavy head came up in a direct challenge. "Yes or no, Charley? It's your big chance. If I bungle it, you take over. You'll be in the saddle. The odds favor you, and you always preferred things that way."

Rudge looked perplexed. This was a Thayer he could not understand. He hadn't thought about the business of the plane and the attendant publicity involved. He would have to learn to think things through like that. But Rudge had no lack of faith in his own strength or destiny. His strange amber eyes were hard and clear.

"All right, we'll go," he said.

Chapter Ten

The wind and rain shifted to the southwest, the west, and then began to abate as it swung into the next quarter. The *Firefly* was a broad-beamed boat, as seaworthy as any of the shrimp fishermen whose lines she followed. She more than held her own against sea and wind on the dark wilderness of the Gulf.

Byrum was at the wheel. His eyes ached. It was an hour before dawn and the time that had passed since boarding the *Firefly* seemed endless. His every bone and muscle protested against the continuing effort to stay alert. In the glow of the binnacle light, his face looked taut and drawn.

Not another light showed in all the vastness of dark water that heaved around them. The land had long ago sunk beneath the black horizon astern.

Clemi sat beside him on the flying bridge of the *Firefly*. She stared toward the east, looking for the dawn. Somehow she had freshened her face and hair, although the bruise and swelling around her mouth where Rudge had hit her was more evident now. Her eyes met his in the glow of the binnacle.

"How long will it take us to reach Guayamas?" she whispered.

He shrugged. "It depends on the weather. The wind is dropping, swinging astern. It might even help us now, even though the *Firefly* tends to roll like a barrel in a following sea."

"How long?" she repeated.

"It's over five hundred miles," he said. "We're doing about eighteen an hour, but we'll have to throttle down to save gas.

Make it about ten miles, average. We'll get there sometime day after tomorrow."

"And fuel?" she asked.

He turned his head. Rudge sat behind him and below, looking up from the main cabin. "The tanks were topped before we left. We're running on about five gallons average now. We'll need plenty to make it."

"The *Firefly's* tanks don't hold enough, do they?"

"No," Byrum said. "Not quite. Thayer's hoping to pick up Steve and Myra tomorrow, long before we run out."

"But suppose we don't?"

"We become derelict, unless—" He shrugged again. "Rudge put that auxiliary tank on the transom. An extra fifty gallons. It might take us there. Or we might meet somebody and borrow some fuel."

"You've never made such a long trip in the *Firefly*, have you?"

"No."

The boat lifted, rolled, and surged forward on the following sea. Byrum watched the compass card wobble in the bowl. He would have to make the whole trip by dead reckoning unless the clouds cleared tomorrow. He knew the tides and winds in the Gulf fairly well, but not well enough to pin-point his way. The entire thing was a gamble, and it came to him that perhaps Thayer was a little insane. The hope of overtaking Steve's boat was less than good. It would be a miracle if they spotted them when dawn came. And Thayer was obviously counting on a miracle.

Rudge had made one more objection to the chase. He had challenged Byrum's story of Steve's destination. He had demanded to know why they should accept it as truth, without checking at all before starting on a wild-goose chase that might end nowhere. Thayer had paused a long moment before replying, studying Byrum and Clemi with hard eyes.

"If Myra isn't in Guayamas, they'll never live to lie again."

"What good would that do? The money will be lost by then."

"Byrum isn't lying," Thayer said. "Are you, Byrum?"

"No."

"You know what happens to Clemi if you are?"

"Yes, I know."

"You don't want to change your story?"

"Steve and Myra said they were going to Guayamas."

Thayer said heavily, "Then you'd better start praying that they don't change their minds."

Thayer sat in his wheelchair in the main cabin below. He seemed to be asleep, leaving the watch to Rudge. He had gotten aboard with the aid of crutches, surprisingly capable when he quit his chair for that brief time. Byrum knew he held a gun under the blanket that covered his legs. Rudge was armed, too, his Luger thrust into his broad leather belt. Serena was asleep in one of the four bunks in the forward compartment. There were no other weapons aboard and Byrum had no illusions about tackling Rudge and taking the man by surprise. Not now, at any rate. Not during these early hours.

The rain slackened and ended as dawn approached, but the seas were still heavy, rolling up under the *Firefly*'s transom and making her motion irregular and uneasy. Byrum looked back at Rudge again. The man had his eyes closed. His mouth worked. He looked ill. Seasick. But not sick enough. Off to the east, a faint pearly light tinged the unsettled horizon, a grayness that was not light or darkness but somewhere in between. He felt Clemi's hand reach across between the two cushioned bucket seats on the bridge and touch his fingers on the wheel.

"Pete?"

"Take it easy. We'll just have to wait and see."

"You told them about Steve because of me," she said quietly. "But don't blame yourself too much. You told me a lot, too, when you did that. You didn't want Rudge to hurt me any more. I love you, Pete."

He nodded. "It goes both ways."

"Does it, Pete?" she whispered.

"I was blind and stupid. I was too busy with the Lodge to see you all these years, Clemi. But when I had to go back into the Navy, I found that all I could think about was you. And now it's too late, isn't it?"

"No," she said. "I'm happier than I ever hoped to be."

"You know what Rudge will have to do with us, don't you? It doesn't matter whether we find Steve and Myra or not; it won't make any difference in what Rudge and Thayer will do to us."

"I know. But I can't believe it. Not right now. I don't want to think about it," Clemi whispered. Her hand stroked his fingers. "I just want to think about you. About you and me, Pete."

He looked back as a sound came from Rudge. The man had opened his eyes and stood up, braced against the narrow sides of the ladder to the bridge. His face was pale and yellow under his tan. His eyes were ill.

"Can't you keep this damn thing on an even keel?"

"We've got a following sea," Byrum said quietly.

"You're doing it on purpose." Rudge sounded petulant. "You want me to get sick. Serena shot off that fat mouth of hers, told you I couldn't swim, didn't she? Well, maybe I can't. But listen, friend—before I go under, you get it. And before you get it, your girl gets it. You like her, don't you? Well, you won't like what I do to her unless you get smart." Rudge wiped the back of his hand across his mouth. "So get smart. Keep this ship on a straight line."

"I'm doing my best," Byrum said quietly.

"It isn't good enough. Just watch it, that's all." Rudge reached up and pulled at Clemi's arm. "You, Clemi. Get down in the galley and make us some breakfast. I put plenty of food aboard before we shoved off on this crazy deal. Get some coffee. We could all do with something to eat."

"All right," Clemi said. She slid off the stool and squeezed past the blond man to vanish down into the main cabin, turning into the galley forward.

Dawn was gray and lifeless, the sea a heaving mass of irregular hills and valleys, spume-flecked, subsiding slowly as the wind died. There were no vessels in view in any quarter. No *Myra T.* What wind remained was chill and raw, but the lowering of its force made the *Firefly* ride easier.

Thayer was awake when Clemi finished preparing breakfast. He had shifted himself from his wheelchair to the bench that ran along the side of the main cabin and braced himself with his crutches. His heavy jowls were blue with beard. Clemi's breakfast consisted of coffee, bacon, and skillets of fried eggs. Byrum was surprised to find himself hungry. Thayer scarcely touched his food. Rudge ate methodically, his eyes on Byrum and Clemi.

Serena woke up and came out of the forward cabin dressed in white shorts and a turtle-neck sweater, her orange-red hair bound with a white ribbon. Her eyes touched Rudge in mockery, then she swung to Byrum.

"Poor Petey, you must be exhausted. Let me handle the wheel for a while."

"Never mind," Rudge objected.

"But he has to sleep sometime," Serena protested. "I can

handle this boat as well as he, I'll bet. All I need is a course to follow." Her smile was a simpering caricature as her eyes met Byrum's. "Clemi can also take the wheel, you know. And Brother, too. After all, we may need Byrum's help later on."

It was arranged that way. Byrum and Clemi went forward into the small cabin and the door was locked upon them, with Serena's giggles coming through the panel. Serena had not bothered to make up the bunk she had used. The cabin was dark and Byrum did not switch on the light in the overhead. Clemi swung toward him in the narrow area between the bunks, her arms slipping around his shoulders, drawing his head down to hers. Her lips were warm and demanding and frightened. Her body trembled. It was the first true kiss they had shared since their quiet confessions of love. It was like nothing Byrum had experienced before.

"Darling, darling . . . what are we going to do?" Her whisper was almost soundless in his ear. "Isn't there anything at all we can do?"

He held her tightly. "We're all right for now."

"But they'll kill us. Once we catch up to Steve and Myra, they won't need you any more. I know they took me along just to keep you in line. If you could somehow get hold of Rudge's gun . . ."

"Sit down, Clemi." He drew her down with him on one of the bunks. She was trembling violently. Her hands that came out of the darkness to touch his face were cold. He kissed her. "I'm in no condition to take on Rudge right now. I've been in the hospital too long. Unless I can take him by surprise, we're done. He'd kill me."

"Perhaps when he gets to sleep . . ."

"And Thayer has a gun with him all the time, too," Byrum added. "Don't let his appearance of being asleep fool you."

"Then what can we do?"

"Watch. And wait," he said. "That's all."

"Suppose we overtake Steve and Myra?"

"I don't think we will," he said.

"Then suppose Steve doesn't actually go to Guayamas?"

He held her gently. "Let's not borrow that sort of trouble until we get there, Clemi. You need rest. So do I."

"Hold me," she whispered. "Hold me tight."

He knew what she was thinking. There might be only these few pitiful minutes together, here in the privacy and darkness of the compartment. He was aware of her and her nearness, and desired her in every cell of his body. At the same moment, he also heard the thrust and slap of the sea against the *Firefly's* bow, and his senses gauged the roll of the hull and measured the steady beat of her twin engines driving her southeast across the turmoil of the Gulf. Footsteps sounded momentarily on the deck overhead, then on the bridge. And then came the measured thump of Thayer's crutches as the other man moved painfully about.

"Pete," Clemi whispered. "Darling . . ."

The clean fragrance of her filled him. He drew her to him and held her tightly in the darkness, and he knew he held everything dear and precious to him in a world that had suddenly exploded in violence and disaster, in destruction of everything he had once thought necessary and desirable . . .

He slept as if he had been drugged, the long hours of exhausting effort behind him like an irresistible weight that dragged him down into soothing darkness. The motion of the boat was easier now, the rhythm of the engines unchanged and monotonous, churning up the nautical miles toward their destination.

Later, he remembered dreaming about the old life, about the old man coming home from the waterfront, tired and dirty, and the nights on the streets with the gang, the poolroom, and then the old man's funeral in the rain. He dreamed of the poker game he ran in New Haven when he was at Yale, and the early days of the Pelican Lodge, when each problem was a challenge and an adventure, when his sole aim was to make it into a fine gambling-dining establishment of respectable stature. Still later, he dreamed of Adam Fahey's dead body. . . .

He awoke all at once, aware of Clemi in the bunk with him. She had drawn the small leather curtains over the ports and the cabin was almost in total darkness except where a small sliver of sunlight leaked through. Sunlight meant that the weather had cleared. He knew he had been asleep for four, maybe six hours, and for several moments he was aware of a fuzziness of thought. He listened to the steady beat of the engines and measured the way the boat plowed through the water.

"Clemi—"

"Hush, sweetie. Relax, darling."

The whispered voice held a suppressed giggle in it. It wasn't Clemi. It was Serena Thayer.

For a moment he was totally confused, not understanding how this could have happened. He was alone in the cabin with her. Because of the beat of the engines and the running sounds of the sea, he could not guess where Thayer or Rudge or Clemi might be.

"Get up," he said thickly.

She pressed against him. "Petey, sweetheart, it's all right, we're alone here. Clemi is up on the bridge with Brother. I sent her up there. Rudge is asleep. Nobody can disturb us. They don't know I slipped in here to be with you."

"Get up," he said again.

"You don't really mean that," she whispered softly. "Not really."

Somebody moved heavily across the deck overhead. It sounded like Rudge's footsteps. Serena did not seem to be aware of anything except Byrum. Her eyes were big and wild, fastened on his face, a slow anger beginning to pinwheel in their depths.

"Nobody ever treated me like this," she whispered thinly.

"You don't care anything for me," Byrum said. "You hate me. You'd like to see me killed, and perhaps you expect to see me die soon. Was that the reason for your visit here? Looking for some kind of new experience?"

"No, no. I just thought—you and I are a lot alike, you know."

He was silent.

"You've always been alone. So have I. We have certain aims in common," Serena whispered.

"Such as?"

"We're going to kill Rudge," she said. She spoke the words in a casual way that carried none of the enormity of murder. "Brother has to get rid of him. And you'll help us."

He was silent.

"Brother and I talked it all over this morning while you and Clemi were down here sleeping. I had to show Rudge how to steer a simple compass course and we left him up on the bridge while we talked it out. Brother and I both know that Rudge is slated to take over everything in Oswanda. We both know what Rudge is. If we don't get that money back, our throats get cut. You understand that, don't you?"

"Yes," Byrum said.

She propped herself up on her elbows, drew a ragged breath, then smiled.

"We decided there's only one simple way out of this mess for all of us. Unless you want to go to the state authorities and cut your own throat. Brother is willing to be fair to you. He doesn't want any trouble. What he wants more than anything is to prove he can handle things quietly, by himself. He wants the money back that Dulaney stole last night. He's got to have that, or New Orleans will chop him off. You can understand that, I'm sure. We can't trust Rudge one single inch. We have to get rid of him and at the same time get the money back from Steve Dulaney. That's why Brother decided to make the trip this way. Rudge is no damned good on a boat. He's terrified of the water. It will be easy enough to handle him when the time comes."

Byrum looked at her. He could not trust or believe anything she said. Yet some of it made sense.

"And where do I fit in?" he asked.

"Brother say he'll let Steve go if we get the money back. You and Clemi can stay in Mexico if you like. We'll squash the thing about that Fahey creature. You won't have the law after you, and Brother won't bother you, either. And we'll give you fifty thousand dollars to call everything square."

"And Thayer keeps the Pelican?"

"Naturally."

"And you came down here to tell me this, to offer this deal?"

"That was one of the reasons, darling. You don't like me, I know. But you really don't know anything at all about me. Have you ever thought of the kind of life I've had to live as the sister of Alton Thayer? Have you?"

"I thought you rather enjoyed it," Byrum said.

"I hate it, and I hate him. I hate everything about Oswanda. It's stupid, frustrating, utterly horrible. If I had any strength at all, I'd have killed Brother long ago. Because that's the only way I figure I can get out of it."

"Where would you rather be?"

She looked up, raising her arms and clasping her hands behind her head to lean back in the bunk. "Anywhere but Oswanda, darling. New York, maybe. Paris, certainly. Or South America. That's the sort of place I really belong. But of course Brother won't ever let me go . . . Oh, I've wanted to kill him for a long, long time. But I don't have the courage."

"What are you getting at, Serena?"

She smiled. "You can kill Rudge for us, darling."

"And your brother next?"

The tip of her tongue touched her lips. "We'll see."

"No," he insisted. "Let's decide now. Do you want me to kill him, too?"

She thought about it, like a child considering a choice of candy. "All right," she said.

"Is that why you really came here?"

"Petey, you don't have to be so crude," she pouted.

"Killing a brother is crude," Byrum said harshly. "Get out."

She was very quiet. It was plain that she had actually expected, from his questions, that he would be willing to go along with what she proposed. A film clouded her eyes and she held her body stiffly.

The *Firefly* lurched unevenly. Someone shouted up on the bridge above and there came a sudden change in the even beat of the boat's engines. The throttles were pushed forward to full speed and the steady rhythm became a bellowing roar as full power was fed to the cylinders. The bow came up and the *Firefly* began planing with a lunging, smashing motion as her course was changed to a diagonal to the seas.

Something had happened up there.

Byrum turned to the door, then halted as Serena stood up from the bunk. Her thin face was calm again.

"I gather your answer is no," she said.

"On every count."

She smiled. "I'll be glad to watch you die, darling."

She pushed past him and went up on deck.

Chapter Eleven

It was a false alarm. The vessel sighted at about four miles to the southeast was not the *Myra T*. When they were still short of hailing distance, Thayer ordered Byrum, who had taken the wheel from Rudge, to return to their former course. There were three couples on the other boat and they waved as the *Firefly* sheered away. For a fleeting moment, Byrum wondered what chance he had if he kept the *Firefly* heading toward the other vessel and shouted for help. It would probably be his last act on earth, he decided. He saw Rudge leaning against the rail, the gun in his hand dangling at his side, out of sight of the other people beyond the sunglinted water. Rudge looked better than he had last night.

It was almost noon and the sun had turned hot again. Clemi, relegated to the galley once more, prepared lunch of Spam and fried potatoes. Thayer drank beer out of the icebox, one can after the other. He had returned to his wheelchair, braced in the cockpit aft, and his gun was in plain sight on his lap.

The sky was a brazen bowl of heat. Now and then they spotted other vessels, but none resembled their quarry. Byrum took the wheel through most of the afternoon. For several hours after lunch, Clemi disappeared below to sleep. She returned with a peaked cap for Byrum and a fresh singlet she had found in his clothes locker. Thayer was still in the stern cockpit, his eyes hooded and unblinking, watching Byrum. Rudge had finally turned in to sleep. Serena lay sunning herself forward, a towel folded in a narrow band over her eyes.

Clemi's tanned face was grave as she joined Byrum.

"What did she want, Pete?"

"Nothing much," he said wryly. "She offered me a job. To kill Rudge, join Thayer, help get his money back—on condition they'll let Steve live."

Clemi's smile was unfathomable. "Is that all?"

"No. There was a special inducement. Herself."

"Oh?" Clemi's smile changed. "Pete, is there any chance we can do something to get out of this?"

"Thayer and Rudge are both armed. I can't handle Rudge alone."

"He's asleep now," Clemi whispered.

Byrum looked at her sharply. She was serious. He grinned and patted her hand. "Lean against me," he said quietly. "Pretend we're billing and cooing."

"That's not difficult."

"Give it a minute or two, then go below and turn the lock on the forward compartment. Don't waken Rudge, whatever you do. When you come back, go directly forward and talk to Serena. Talk about anything."

A white fishing boat was off the port beam perhaps a mile away, and the smudge from a tanker's funnel made a gray streak against the horizon forward. The seas had grown quiet and serene. Byrum pulled out the choke of the star-board engine a half inch and listened to the suddenly changed, laboring sound as the rhythm was broken. Clemi was pale as she kissed his cheek and left him. He waited, giving her time to get below. Tension built up in him.

He turned abruptly, hearing the starboard engine cough and sputter with too much choke, and dropped down the ladder toward the stern cockpit where Thayer sat in his wheelchair beyond the engine hatches.

Thayer's eyes were dark and cold.

"What is it?" he asked deeply.

"Some adjustment out of whack. I'll look at it."

"How much fuel have we left?"

"I think we'll make it," Byrum said truthfully.

He took the cover off the starboard hatch and stared down at the laboring Northrop engine. Exhaust fumes were heavy from the starboard pipe. The *Firefly* plodded easily ahead on the course he had set. The tanker was hull down on the horizon. The sun felt like an iron fist on the back of his neck as he bent over the open hatch.

Thayer's voice came from behind him. "Serena tells me you turned down my offer."

"Sure," Byrum said easily. "No deal."

"Are you stupid? Or just crazy?"

"Neither."

"Stubborn, perhaps. So stubborn you'll likely die of it," Thayer said quietly. "I've got to get that money back, you understand. I want Myra, too. All the rest, I'm willing to forgive and forget."

"And the little matter of Fahey's murder?"

"We throw Rudge to the wolves for it."

"So you'll be top apple again?"

"A man does what he has to do. It's too late for me to start looking around for another job. Not that the people who finance me will let me go on. You and I are both faced with the same thing, Mr. Byrum. Death. One way or another, when we finish this cruise things will be settled for both of us."

Byrum opened a tool locker beside the engine hatch and took out a wrench. He saw from the tail of his eye that Thayer held his big Colt steadily in the hand resting on the arm of his chair. But the gun was not pointed directly at him. Serena still lolled on her back on the deck, out of sight beyond the bridge.

Clemi came up out of the hatch and nodded her blond head slightly, the sunlight tangled in her hair. Her eyes were grave.

Byrum bent over the engine, wrench in hand. Thayer sat six feet behind him and a little to the left. Under his arm he saw the man look at Clemi as she came aft—and with a quick flip, Byrum flung the wrench at Thayer.

The heavy spanner struck Thayer in the upper arm and clattered to the deck. The heavy gun in his hand went off with a crash, the bullet spinning high into the air. Byrum turned and drove for the man in the wheelchair. He got his hand on the Colt and slammed it to the arm of the chair. Thayer's heavy face convulsed. The gun went off again and Byrum felt the jolt of the recoil through Thayer's thick wrist. The bullet went wide, spitting into the sea beyond the *Firefly's* rail. Byrum bore down with all his weight, twisting the gun. Thayer cursed and writhed in his chair, but the gun came loose. Thayer drove his left into Byrum's stomach. He felt the jolt of pain like a wall of fire. The gun hit the deck and skittered quickly aside.

Clemi darted forward and snatched it up.

Byrum moved back from the wheelchair.

"Give me the gun, Clemi."

She handed it to him, looking forward for Serena.

"Did you lock the door?"

"Yes. Rudge didn't stir."

"He's moving around now," Byrum said grimly. He looked at Thayer. The man in the wheelchair had shoved himself backward against the opposite rail. His face reflected pure animal rage. Byrum was grateful for the weight and solidity of the gun in his hand. He turned and started forward. "Take care of Serena," he told Clemi. "Keep her on the forward deck. Can you manage?"

"Yes," she said quickly.

"Go ahead."

There was only Rudge left; the killer's Luger to be accounted for. But he had a gun of his own now and Rudge was in the forward cabin behind the locked door. The door was flimsy; the lock accounted for nothing.

Byrum eased forward through the main deckhouse cabin. Three steel-edged stairs led down to the shutter door that closed off the sleeping compartment. He stood above the little well, checking the latch Clemi had thrown shut.

"Rudge!" he called.

There was no answer.

He looked back and saw that Clemi had already gone forward to the bridge.

"Rudge, come out of there."

Still no answer.

Then he heard a small scraping sound, a thump, another scraping.

Forward, he heard Clemi's scream.

Byrum snapped up the bar latch, kicked the louvered door open and plunged into the stateroom. It was a mistake. Another hatchway led to the forward head and storage compartment, and this door stood wide open. Sunlight streamed through a second hatch in the forward deck. At once, he knew that Rudge had wakened with the shots, tried the door and then found his way forward and up through the deck hatch where Serena had been sun-bathing. Rudge was up there now, armed and ready, while he had trapped himself in the place where Rudge had been.

Byrum plunged aft again. He was halfway across the main cabin when he heard Clemi scream a second time.

"Pete, help!"

His mouth went dry with fear.

He saw Thayer in his wheelchair on the afterdeck. The big gray man was staring at the deck over Byrum's head. So Rudge was up there. Byrum waited. He saw Thayer nod his head suddenly, his gaze dropping level to meet Byrum's eyes. Thayer could see him in the shadows of the cabin. But nothing changed in the man's harshly lined face. He gave no hint as to what outcome he hoped for in this impasse.

"Byrum!"

Rudge's shout was a thunderclap, strong and arrogant. "Byrum, throw out your gun!"

"Come and get it," Byrum called softly.

He heard Rudge's deep laughter. "I don't have to, friend. I've got your girl up here with my gun in her back. You want me to pull the trigger?"

Byrum felt sweat start out all over him. The Colt in his hand felt slippery.

"Clemi?"

He heard her thin gasp.

He looked at Thayer. Thayer nodded confirmation. Byrum felt the heavy weight of defeat and despair.

"All right," he called. "Send her to Thayer where I can see her. You can keep her covered that way."

Rudge hesitated, then called down agreement. Byrum heard Clemi's stumbling footsteps and a moment later she came into view, coming down the ladder to the stern cockpit with Thayer. She looked disheveled and one side of her face was discolored. Byrum swallowed an acid taste in the back of his throat.

He threw out the gun. It clattered on the deck, glinting in the hot sunlight. The *Firefly* lifted and fell, and he became aware of the fact that the engines had been slowed to idle. That would be Serena at the helm, adjusting the choke he had deliberately fouled in order to get near Thayer

"Come on out!" Rudge called.

Byrum stepped out of the shadows of the cabin, his hand

at his sides. He turned to face forward, looking up. Rudge stood there, legs spread for balance against the motion of the boat. He looked enormous, a black shadow against the dazzling blue of the sky above.

Rudge laughed. For a moment Byrum saw imminent death in his eyes. Then Rudge jumped lightly down to the cockpit and scooped up the gun. Thayer's lips looked tight and bloodless. Rudge pocketed the Colt and moved toward Byrum with the light, graceful step of a huge cat.

"Is this what Serena put you up to?" he asked softly. A small smile twitched the corners of his mouth. He looked as dangerous as a spitting tiger. "Is this why she crawled into your bunk this morning?"

Byrum said nothing.

"Thayer thinks he can knock me off this trip. Maybe he made a deal with you. Is that it?"

"No. There was no deal."

"But that's what Thayer suggested, isn't it?"

Thayer spoke from his wheelchair. "Let it go, Charley." His voice was weary. "He didn't get away with it. Give me my gun."

Rudge laughed. "So you can turn it on me now? Then toss me to the sharks?"

"Don't be a fool," Thayer snapped. "We can settle our personal differences when we get to Mexico and find the money."

"From now on," Rudge said flatly, "I'm running this boat. You take orders from me, Al. You jump when I tell you to. Understand?"

Thayer's lips were thin. "I won't forget this."

A flush of rage darkened Rudge's handsome features. "You made a deal with Byrum to get rid of me. You think I didn't have my ear to the deck while that sister of yours sneaked into Byrum's bunk? You started it, but I'm finishing it. If you don't like it, you can walk home." Abruptly he swung back to Byrum. "As for you, you might get ideas again before we're through. So just to teach you how to behave—"

Rudge was smiling. The next instant Byrum felt the incredible impact of the gun across his face, and explosion of pain that drove him back until his legs hit the engine hatch and he fell over it.

Dimly he heard Clemi scream.

As he straightened, with sky and sea reeling before him, he saw Rudge's figure, huge against the hot blue sky, and his arm was knocked aside as Rudge hit him again. And then once more. He fell on hands and knees to the deck. He shook his head and blood spattered the mahogany planking in a fine bright spray.

He was aware of nothing but the agony of his pain. Then he felt Rudge's shoe pushing at his ribs, and he fell over and saw Rudge step in once more, his outline dark and terrible against a blaze of light that burst into proportions beyond belief.

Chapter Twelve

He had been adrift on a starless sea for a long time —he could not guess how long he had been unconscious or how long he had slept afterward—but his eyes opened to the night and he lay still, testing the pain that flooded his face and surged from bruises all through his body.

He felt the bunk under him, sensed the steady forward thrust of the *Firefly* through the long swells of the Gulf. The curtains had been pulled aside over the ports and he stared out at the night in some surprise, glimpsing the phosphorescent reflection of the moon on the black sea.

A shadow stirred beside him and a cold compress was placed against the throbbing pain in his face. In the dimness he saw Clemi kneeling beside his bunk. She wore one of his khaki shirts, taken from his clothing locker, the sleeves rolled up on her slim arms. She had also borrowed a pair of his dungarees, and she looked altogether like a child masquerading in adult clothing. Her whisper was almost inaudible.

"Pete?"

"I'm all right, Clemi."

"You're not. It was awful. It was all my fault. I couldn't stop Rudge from coming up out of the hatch. I yelled to you. Didn't you hear?"

He shook his head, and the pain throbbed and then receded to less than it had been. "No, not until it was too late."

"Never mind," she said. "Never mind it now."

"Who's running the *Firefly*?"

"They're taking turns. Serena has the wheel now. Thayer is drunk—he finished all the beer. Rudge has been awful. He acts like he was a—god or something. A dark devil god. I'm afraid of him, Pete."

"Any idea where we are?"

"More than halfway, I'd guess."

"How is the fuel?"

"Rudge checked the fuel himself. He cut the speed down to save on it. We'll make it, Pete. But then what?"

"We'll see," Byrum said. He propped himself up and a wave of dizziness made him pause until it passed. "There hasn't been any sign of the *Myra*?"

"No."

"What do you know about this town they're heading for?"

"Guayamas? It's just a little fishing village."

"Why did Steve choose it?"

"He bought some property there. It's just a little place, with a tiny harbor and a *posada* that gets a few tourists who wander out that way. Steve bought a house on the beach west of town. I think even then he was planning to do this, Pete, and he wanted a place to hide until he could make the next jump, perhaps to South America."

"You think he planned this all long ago with Myra?"

"I—I'm afraid so."

"Is he well known in Guayamas?"

"He's only been there two or three times."

Byrum was silent, groping for something, anything at all, to pin his hopes on. He started to rise from the bunk and he staggered and had to lean heavily upon Clemi. Her whisper was concerned.

"Please, darling. Please. Just rest. As long as Rudge doesn't bother you, stay down here until you feel better."

"I'm all right now."

"Let me get you some food," she said quickly. "I can heat a can of soup and some coffee."

He felt the welts and bruises on his face. His mouth was swollen and several teeth felt loose. "And a couple of aspirin for dessert," he muttered.

"In a minute," Clemi said. "Just stay here. Please. Rudge is too dangerous right now. There's no telling what he might do if you came up on deck now."

"What about Thayer and Serena?"

Clemi said bitterly, "Serena is having the time of her life. Somehow she doesn't even give a thought to the fact that Rudge will kill her, too. And Thayer hasn't said a word, or made any attempt to get out of his wheelchair. He's still back there where you saw him—he didn't move all afternoon."

"What time is it now?"

"Almost ten o'clock. Now lie down, darling. I'll be right back."

He had one more hour of rest before Rudge came below and ordered him to take the wheel. The man looked bigger, more decisive than before. He kept his gun in hand and Byrum did not see the Colt he had taken from Thayer. He took Serena's place at the helm and Rudge ordered her astern to stay with her brother.

The night was still and clear. The Gulf had grown calm and the water had a glasslike quality under the half-moon that rode in the hot black sky. There was no wind. Now and then they spotted the running lights of another boat, once passing a yawl under canvas that rolled, sails slatting idly, in the calm. The yawl was like a ghost, her sails pale against the sky, a few dim lights showing in her cabin ports. Nobody came on deck to hail them and in a few minutes she was far astern. Serena had left cigarettes on the shelf above the controls and Byrum helped himself to one as he watched the other vessel vanish. He felt better; the aspirin had dulled the throb in his face.

Rudge was a silent, massive figure in the seat opposite him. His head was thrust forward a little as if to help his eyes pierce the night gloom ahead.

Byrum dragged at the cigarette. "There's a lot of hell popping in Oswanda right now."

"How is that?"

"Sheriff Jergens has probably found Fahey's body by now. I left it under Flo Gilligan's house. Jergens isn't altogether stupid."

"So what?"

"That makes it a public case. Questions are going to be asked in all sorts of places—the newspapers, the D.A.'s office, in New Orleans, too."

"Jergens will cover it," Rudge said shortly.

"Maybe. But you're missing and so is Thayer. Jergens might think you've all skipped and left him holding the bag. He might act like a real cop for a change. By the way, what did you do with Flo Gilligan?"

"She's been paid off."

"Did you kill her?" Byrum asked quietly.

Rudge grunted. "She's in New Orleans. Our people put her in a hotel. They're watching her. She won't get a chance to step out of line."

"I see. What do you plan to do if the Coast Guard stops us, Rudge?"

The blond man turned his narrow head sharply to stare at Byrum. "The Coast Guard? Why should they come into it?"

"I was just trying to picture the situation in Oswanda." Byrum shrugged. "Thayer's boat is gone, right after Steve Dulaney breaks out of jail. Steve and Myra Thayer disappear together. I'm seen by Jergens helping Steve crash out, and I've disappeared, too. Then my boat vanishes. Jergens is found locked in Steve's cell. Even he won't be able to keep that from the public. They might send a plane or boats out to hunt for us."

"Hell," Rudge said. "It's a big ocean."

"But you don't know much about it, do you?"

There was a sudden uncertainty in the big man. He stood up in anger, then sat down again, twisted in the seat to stare at Byrum. The gun was loose in his hand, but Byrum had no illusions about Rudge's readiness to use it if he made a play for it.

"What are you getting at?" Rudge asked softly.

"Thayer hates you. He's afraid of you. Maybe he figures he doesn't have much to lose by calling copper on you. He's ready to throw you to the wolves, anyway, because you plan to step into his shoes. Well, there's a radio in the main cabin below. Serena knows all about boats even if you don't. She knows how to work the radio. Maybe she's called for help already."

Rudge expelled a breath of relief and chuckled. "Hell, I smashed that first thing, friend. Are you trying to worry me?"

There was a sharp edge to Rudge's voice that warned Byrum into silence again. Rudge was on edge, keyed to a high pitch of tension that had brought him to the brink of explosive violence. His nerves were strained to the breaking point by his overt challenge of Thayer's control in Oswanda and by the knowledge that this trip would end in final victory for one or the other. Added to that was his terror of the sea. His fear was evident in the tight-lipped way in which he surveyed the black night through which the *Firefly* plowed, in his knowledge that he couldn't swim, and in all the landsman's fears, real and imaginary, of the threats inherent in this watery world he couldn't master.

At midnight, Clemi brought Byrum coffee and offered to relieve him. Rudge ordered her off the bridge. Thayer and

Serena remained aft. The night was warm and cloudless, the sea calm. Byrum's face began to ache worse than before and at times he felt quick spasms of nausea. He belonged in bed for the next day or two.

He was caught between Thayer and Rudge, both men hating each other, struggling for stakes in the jungle in which they lived. There was always Clemi and the overwhelming importance of keeping her safe. He wanted her, for always.

The hours of night slid by in monotony, with Rudge gulping hot coffee mixed with brandy from a flask he kept for himself. His eyes searched sky and sea nervously, as if Byrum's words about potential pursuit had fastened in his mind with talons of fear. The day dawned clear. Now and then they passed shrimp boats out of Gulf ports and the Tortugas, and once Rudge abruptly ordered Byrum to steer within hailing distance of one and then Rudge called out to learn if the other vessel had spotted the *Myra T.* There was some discussion among the fishermen, but the captain bellowed back that no boat like that had passed in their sight. Rudge grunted and ordered Byrum back on course.

At ten o'clock Byrum prevailed on Rudge to let him check the fuel tanks, and he discovered that both regular tanks were all but empty. He switched to auxiliary and kept the throttle at slow cruising speed. It wouldn't be long now before the bank of clouds on the southern horizon materialized into the coast of Mexico. Consulting his charts, he corrected course for drift and tide, and hoped he would not be too far off target. His growing fatigue made his thinking unreliable and he did not try to make his compass corrections too exact.

It was after two in the afternoon before the Mexican coast became defined to the south. Another hour and they were five miles offshore, searching for landmarks. Byrum had no record in his pilot books of the village of Guayamas. Apparently it was too insignificant to be noted in the American charts he carried aboard the *Firefly.* It was Alton Thayer who gave unexpected aid in the problem.

Thayer rolled up his wheelchair to where he could be seen from the bridge and hailed Byrum. "You're ten miles west of the spot we want. Just follow the coast and keep well offshore. Guayamas has a small harbor, one long wharf with a shed on it, and a cannery with a large stack on a hill above the town. Look for the stack. You can't miss it."

"How do you know it so well?" Byrum asked.

"I've been here before," Thayer said grimly. "In the old

days when we made the alky runs. Just like shuttling a ferry."

Rudge picked up his binoculars and scanned the coast. His gun rested on the shelf before him, near his left hand. Byrum rubbed a hand over his battered mouth, aware of the bristles of his beard. He had not shaved in two days. He looked unkempt and disreputable.

Clemi came up on the bridge to stand beside him. Rudge did not object. Her hand rested on Byrum's shoulder and he felt the tension trembling in her. Their glances met in despair and they both studied the shore that slid slowly past the *Firefly's* beam.

Most of the coast was wild, a green jungle that lifted in a series of folded hills toward the island's spine. A few fishing boats worked farther out to sea, and once, through a gap in the hills, Byrum saw the glint of steel rails and heard the faint toylike whistle of a locomotive. The jog eastward took thirty minutes. Rudge began to whistle thinly between his teeth as he kept sweeping the shore with the binoculars.

"There it is," Thayer announced. He rolled his chair back from the rail, his face gray in the harsh sunlight. "Rudge, you'd better give me my gun."

"You're not going anywhere," Rudge said.

"I want Steve Dulaney for myself."

"Get this straight, Al." Rudge grinned. "I don't give a damn about your wife or settling your private scores. I'm here to get the money back. What you do about your wife is your own business. You can take care of it later."

"You've got to help me," Thayer said harshly.

Rudge fixed the crippled man with a cold gaze. A muscle jumped in his jaw. "You still don't understand do you? I've taken over, Al. You don't get another chance to dump me. And you're not getting back to Oswanda."

"What is that supposed to mean?"

"You can figure it out with no strain."

Thayer whispered, "But the board in New Orleans—"

"I'm their boy. They'll back me—especially when I clean up the mess you made and get their money into their hot, greedy pads."

"But you're the one who killed Fahey—"

"Nobody knows that but us little mice on this boat." Rudge's eyes were hard and tight. "Now shut up, Al, you hear?"

The harbor of Guayamas opened before the *Firefly's* bow. It was little more than an inlet, open to the north and east, with a low promontory on the west and a shelving beach in front of a cluster of shacks and stucco houses on the fringe of the jungle wilderness. Several fishing boats were pulled up on the pebbly beach and a single wharf stuck out into the shallow harbor. Beyond the wharf was the cannery, with a tall stack of red brick that partly obscured a pale blue building bearing the painted legend, POSADA GUAYAMAS. The town looked blasted by the crushing heat of the afternoon sun. Byrum glimpsed a small plaza fronting the *posada,* a church with a low belfry, market stalls, and a few cantinas. The cannery seemed deserted at the moment.

There was only one other boat in the harbor besides the fishing smacks pulled up on the beach. Tied to the cannery wharf was the *Myra T.*

Rudge exhaled softly. "Slow down, Byrum. Get me alongside."

Clemi whispered, "I hoped they wouldn't really be here."

"You're lucky you didn't get your wish, sister," Rudge said bleakly. "It wouldn't have been so good for you if that boat wasn't here."

There was no sign of life aboard the other yacht as they drifted alongside the cannery pier. On the beach nearby, two men came out of a shack festooned with drying seine nets and watched idly, bare feet curled on the hot pebbles. The fishermen wore only ragged white cotton trousers and floppy straw hats. The *Myra* was silent. Her fifty-foot length gleamed with expensive chrome and brass fittings; her cutter bow nosed gently into the tide. The wide cabin windows, framed in teak, looked empty. Byrum reversed the engines and Serena, astern with Thayer, made a line fast to the other boat. Serena looked thin and angry. Rudge weighed the Luger in his hand.

"All of you stay here except Clemi," he said. "She comes with me. That's just so you won't get the idea of beaching me, Byrum."

Clemi, pale and silent, boarded the *Myra* with Rudge moving like a stalking cat behind her. Tension curled in Byrum. But there was nothing he could do. The sun winked on Rudge's gun as he gestured Clemi ahead into the cabin. They disappeared. On the beach, the two fishermen turned and walked away toward the main square of the village. The sun was very hot. The fishermen moved at an unusually fast pace.

A minute went by. Another.

Clemi reappeared on the stern deck, Rudge behind her. "They're not here," she called.

Chapter Thirteen

Rudge stood squinting his eyes against the glare of the setting sun. Clemi stepped across the rail to reboard the *Firefly*. In Byrum's shirt and dungarees, she looked like a slim blond boy. Her eyes met Byrum's with a curiously swift warning expression. A dirty yellow fishing boat chugged into the harbor, the blunt bow pushing an oily wave that made the *Firefly* rock heavily against the sides of the deserted *Myra*. Rudge, with one foot awkwardly over the rail, balanced precariously against the unexpected motion of the boats in the wash of the wake.

Now, Byrum thought.

Rudge's arm was raised as he stumbled over the rail and his gun shone in the sunlight. Byrum jumped. He came down from the bridge overhead, his knees slamming into the big man's chest, driving Rudge back across the gap between the two rocking boats. The crushing impact of his weight made Rudge grunt as he slammed off balance to the deck beyond. Byrum twisted as he fell, glimpsing Clemi as she circled Rudge's scrambling figure. Byrum came up fast, grabbing for the gun, flipping it free. A heavy fist slammed into him and Rudge wriggled aside, trying to get free of the narrow deck area between the rail and the main cabin housing. Serena's voice was a keening scream from the *Firefly*. Byrum saw Clemi snatch up the gun he had broken from Rudge's grip. But Rudge was on his feet, teeth gleaming in the sun, his hand on the second gun in his belt. Byrum struck hard, struck again, and Rudge slammed against the rail. A scream of terror burst from him as he saw his peril too late. He landed with a heavy splash in the water between the two boats and sank from sight under the oily surface of the harbor.

Byrum straightened painfully, gasping for breath. Clemi came up to look for Rudge. The two yachts had drifted momentarily apart and Rudge's head broke through to the surface, preceded by his hand and gun upthrust into the air. A strangled shout came from him and he grabbed for the mooring line that held the *Firefly* to the *Myra*. Byrum could see the convulsive jerk of the man's trigger finger as he tried to fire his wet gun. Nothing happened. His head vanished again and only the gun was visible in his hand, still thrust up out of the water.

"Are you all right?" Clemi gasped.

He nodded, drew a deep, aching breath and moved along the rail to search for Rudge. He could kill the man now and maybe that would be best. He reached for the mooring line that kept Rudge's thrashing figure afloat. It would be simple to let him drown, here and now.

Clemi said quickly, "No, Pete. We need him for the police."

He watched Rudge coldly, still moved by his anger. Rudge would have killed him if the situation were reversed. But now he was aware of Clemi's restraining hand on his arm as Rudge pulled himself painfully around the *Firefly's* bow and splashed out of sight. Rudge was trying to haul himself back up on the *Firefly's* deck from the starboard side.

His hesitation was almost fatal. Byrum had forgotten Thayer and Serena.

The shot came as a total surprise. Serena had a small .28 revolver winking in her narrow hand. The sound it made was a flat cracking noise certainly not heard beyond the sun-blasted shingle and the deserted wharf. Splinters flew from the teak trim of the cabin behind him. He pushed Clemi ahead of him around the corner of the deck housing. Clemi stumbled. She still had the Luger she had snatched up, but now she dropped it. With a small scraping sound, it slid over the side into the water.

The threat from Rudge was forgotten.

There was something about Serena's posture, the way her feet were spread on the *Firefly's* deck, that was utterly implacable. Her red hair seemed to flame in an aureole around her thin savage face.

She fired again, and Byrum shoved Clemi toward the wharf. "Run," he gasped.

They were on the dock now, with the corrugated tin shed at their backs. It seemed a long way toward the land end of the wharf as they raced for safety. He heard Serena's scream of anger and another bullet smashed past his head.

The corner of the wharf shed beckoned. Clemi rounded it first, then Byrum. They stood with their backs against the corrugated tin wall, gasping for breath. They were free. For this moment, they were rid of both Rudge and Thayer. And somewhere nearby was Steve Dulaney and Myra.

Serena did not follow them. There were no more shots. No alarm had been raised in the village. The green jungle above the pastel houses and wooden shacks was a dark wall in the setting sun. The heat of the land after two days at sea was oppressive.

Byrum said, "Come along, Clemi."

The long shadow of the church and its belfry lay across the rough cobblestones of the plaza. At the Posada Guayamas, the innkeeper was sprinkling water and sweeping dust from the sun-baked area where he set out his tables. With sundown, the little village was coming to life. A few cars were in evidence, most of ancient vintage, but one or two relatively new Chevrolets, painted a bright red. Somewhere in one of the cantinas a radio blared repetitive Latin rhythms, interspersed with the quick spate of commercials from Mexico City. A group of men in white seersuckers gathered at the tables in front of the *posada* smoked and drank beer and talked in low tones. Nobody paid much attention to Byrum and Clemi as they came out of the side street from the beach.

"How do we go about finding Steve?" she asked.

Byrum sat down at a table removed from the other men in front of the *posada*. He looked back down the narrow street that led to the waterfront, but there was no sign of pursuit from the wharf. He wondered briefly if Rudge had regained the *Firefly's* deck. Even if Rudge had been successful, he would have climbed straight into the muzzle of Serena's gun.

"If Steve bought or rented a house around here, the locals will know about him, right off."

Clemi nodded.

He ordered Crystal beer from the *posadero*, a fat man who sweated heavily in the sultry evening heat. Clemi somehow managed to look prim and neat in her makeshift costume. Byrum looked ragged and disheveled. The *posadero* seemed to be in a hurry. He pulled away when Byrum first spoke to him and when he brought the beer he started off again at once.

"One moment, *senor*," Byrum said in Spanish.

"I am very busy now. Can you not see I have other customers?"

"I only wish a little information," Byrum said quietly. "About the *norteamericano*, *Senor* Dulaney, who recently purchased property in Guayamas."

The fat innkeeper looked across the square. His hands moved nervously. "I know of no such man."

"He arrived today in the yacht tied up to the cannery wharf."

"I did not see him, *senor*."

He turned away irritably and vanished inside the *posada*. Byrum was puzzled. Again he checked down the street toward the waterfront. Nobody had followed them yet. A string of colored lights came on over the area where they sat. The shadows were deep violet in front of the church across the plaza. Then a car came downhill on the single road that led inland from the town, bumping across the cobbled plaza where a flock of scrawny chickens ran, squawking, to escape the wheels. The red Chevrolet sedan paused in front of the inn, rocking on its springs.

Myra Thayer got out.

Byrum remembered the two fishermen on the beach who had watched the *Firefly* enter the harbor. They had run off through the evening heat into town. It was plain that Steve had paid them to watch for pursuit. He stood up, and Myra saw him and walked quickly toward their table.

"Pete. Clemi."

She spoke as if greeting them at a tea party. Her small trim figure was sheathed in white silk and she wore a strip of matching silk in her black, lustrous hair. The deep shadows under her eyes were gone. Her lips smiled. She had lost her fear, exchanging it for a warm security and happiness in the two days she had spent with Steve Dulaney. There was a new assurance in the way she moved and walked, a shining deep in her dark eyes.

"You two look as if you've been camping out for a week," she said. "Pablo told us your boat was in the harbor and I came straight out."

"Where is Steve?"

"Making arrangements about the plane."

"Are you leaving here?" Byrum asked.

"Of course. Tonight. This was only our first stop." She looked quickly from Clemi to Byrum. "What is it? Did anything go wrong back in Oswanda?"

Byrum said flatly, "We didn't come here alone. Thayer, his sister, and Rudge are on the *Firefly*. They'll all be along soon enough."

She stared, not understanding. "But why did you tell them—"

"It wasn't our choice," Clemi said. "They forced us to tell them where you and Steve were going."

The color suddenly drained from Myra's face. In an instant, her appearance changed. "You know about—the money?"

"I came to get it back," Byrum said.

"But you can't— Oh, Pete, you're angry—"

"Did you expect anything else?"

She looked from Byrum to Clemi. In this fragment of time, her small face turned anxious and harried again. Her mouth trembled. "I know how it must seem to you—after all you did for us. I wanted Steve to tell you what he planned to do, but he was afraid you would object or do something to stop us. All we want is a little time to be free, to enjoy a few hours of happiness—"

"On stolen money?" he asked.

"It belongs to Steve as much as to Thayer."

"By that reckoning, it belongs to Pete, too," Clemi said.

Myra looked uncertain. The men in white seersuckers at the other end of the patio were watching them curiously. One of them said something and another laughed softly. It was growing dark in the little village. Uneasiness rode Byrum. He still didn't know what had happened back on the boat. If Rudge was alive or dead, or if Rudge had come to terms with Alton Thayer.

"Let's go talk it over with Steve," he said.

Myra nodded soberly. "I'll drive you there."

The house was to the west of Guayamas, reached by a narrow graveled road that followed the shore for half a mile then cut across a low jungled promontory of cabbage palms to reach more open beaches beyond. The house was new, low and white and modern, with a red-tiled roof and a terrace overlooking a small cliff that edged a gorge, into which the sea licked with an angry tongue on the rocks below. It was dark when they arrived, but lights gleamed behind drawn curtains at the windows. Several times during the brief ride, Byrum glanced back along the primitive road to see if they were being followed. But no headlights pursued them.

Myra parked the car and led the way along the stone patio, one hand on the wooden rail that guarded against the sheer drop of fifty feet onto the tidal rocks below. In the light of the rising moon, the sea to the north gleamed with silver. There was a light wind blowing from inland, bringing with it the heavy odors of the wild palmetto jungles. Byrum wished he could have seen this place in full daylight.

Steve Dulaney stepped out at the sound of the approaching car. He looked tall and slender, like a steel whip, outlined against the light from inside the house, his blond hair silvery in the moon's radiance. His white shirt was open at the collar and he wore dark slacks and sandals. He carried a rifle in his hand.

"Myra? Pete?" Then he saw Clemi and his welcoming grin broadened. "You, too, Sis?"

Myra said in a strange voice, "They've come for the money, Steve. They want to give it back. And they told Thayer where we were. Thayer is somewhere down in the harbor. Serena and Rudge are with him."

Her voice was not quite an accusation of treachery, but Steve's narrow, aristocratic face lost its look of welcome and he scowled. "I don't understand."

"It's simple enough," Byrum said. "Rudge caught Clemi and me and began to push Clemi around. So I told them about Guayamas. Then we all came out here on the *Firefly*. We managed to get away from them in the harbor, but we don't have any time to spare. They'll be right behind us."

"So soon," Myra whispered.

Steve put his arm around her, his rifle lowered. "It's all right. We only need a half hour. The plane will be ready then. Come inside, everybody."

A sea broke thunderously in the gorge below as Byrum followed the others into the house. The living room had a terrazzo floor and modern, angular furniture. It looked impersonal, like a house designed for seasonal rentals. Two suitcases stood just inside the front door, together with a heavily grained briefcase. Steve's trenchcoat lay on one of the suitcases. Steve leaned his rifle against the wall near the luggage and lit a cigarette.

"We have enough time for a drink, haven't we, Pete?"

"I doubt it," Byrum said.

"Don't you want to drink with me, partner?" Steve smiled his charming, reckless smile. "You're not really sore at me, are you, Pete?"

"You put me in a hole back in Oswanda and buried me," Byrum said. He felt a churning distaste for what he had to do but he drove on. "You sold out my share of the Pelican while I was in the Pacific, you got me to pull you out of jail and make a fugitive of myself, you left me holding the bag, charged with Fahey's murder. It never occurred to you to help in that. I can't go back now, any more than you."

"Of course not," Steve said quickly. "You're coming with us."

"You didn't invite us back in Oswanda. You left Clemi and me waiting on the corner."

"We couldn't make it, Petey. Jergens was hot on our heels. But we knew you'd manage to follow us. And you did."

Byrum went on. "I had a chance to clean things up back

in Oswanda. I wanted to make a new start for myself and for Clemi."

"You and Clemi?" Steve's smile broadened. "You mean the scales finally fell from your eyes? Clemi has worshipped you for years, Pete. I can't tell you how glad I am—"

"Shut up," Byrum said. "Shut up and listen. I got the ledgers away from Maury Harris and I was going to turn them over to the Attorney General as evidence of what Thayer had done to Pelican Lodge. It meant taking the rap myself for the illegal gambling I started there, but I didn't really mind that if it cleaned Thayer and the syndicate out of town. The Lodge gambling was my idea. I ran it. I persuaded you and Clemi to accept it even when Clemi objected years ago. Whatever sentence they threw at me would be worth it, just to get a fresh start. But you wrecked any chance I had when you stole Thayer's money for your honeymoon with Myra."

"Now, look, Pete, that money isn't really Thayer's—"

"Nor is it yours to steal," Byrum snapped. "I've come to take it back to the authorities."

"You mean give it back to Thayer's syndicate?" Dulaney's voice was suddenly ugly. "Use it to buy peace with Thayer's mob?"

"I told you my intentions. I want to set the record straight, once and for all." Byrum was keenly aware of the rifle Dulaney held. "I don't care what you and Myra do with your lives from here on. You and Myra can have a running start in your plane to whatever private hell you've chosen for yourselves. But Clemi and I are going back to Oswanda. If I thought I could persuade you to come back with us and help straighten things out, I would try. But I know you're set on running. I'm sorry for you, Steve. For you, too, Myra. I don't doubt that you love each other and need each other. But you're reaching in the wrong direction. You can't run forever. I learned that. I've been running a long time from something I never wanted to face. What I was as a kid, what I might have been. Well, I've stopped running now. I'm going back. And I'm taking the money with me."

As he spoke, Byrum felt as if a great truth had suddenly burst into bright consciousness within himself. He remembered his father, work-weary and broken, big-fisted, a giant whose strength had been eroded by years of disappointments. He remembered the streets he had roamed as a boy, the jungle in which he had lived and received his first education. There was the rain that fell on his father's grave that day and his silent promise to himself to carve a different world for himself, taking an easier path. He had shunned a professional career at law and driven straight for what he assumed to be the simplest way, by using his skill at cards, his temperament for gambling, to get what he thought he wanted. Now it was all ashes.

He looked at Clemi and saw in her face everything he had missed. Her eyes met his with warm promise. Now was the time to pay. The price was worth the promise. He knew this when he looked at her. The past was done and would be paid for. The future could be started with a clean slate.

It depended on Steve.

Steve's face was arrogant, handsome, defiant and unreal.

"You must be off your rocker, Petey, boy," he said softly. "I've gone through too much for that bundle of cash. I planned it too carefully to throw it away on your say-so."

"Then I'll have to take it from you," Byrum said.

"No."

"Put down your rifle, Steve."

"Stay where you are. I'd hate to have to use it."

Through the open door came the sound of the sea smashing into the gorge below the patio. Clemi made a small sound of dismay. Myra, her figure small and trim in white silk, moved closer to Dulaney's tall figure.

"Is the money in the briefcase?" Byrum asked.

"Yes. And in twenty minutes, maybe less, my pilot will arrive. He had a little trouble with the engine. The airfield is only ten minutes from here. We're flying south, Myra and me. Down Central America, maybe into South America. We haven't really decided on our ultimate destination. And under the circumstances," Steve said, smiling grimly, "I don't trust you or Clemi with that knowledge."

Byrum said again, "Put down the gun, Steve."

He started across the room toward the tall man and the luggage.

He saw the rifle come up in Steve's hand, watched the black eye of the muzzle level at his stomach.

Steve's face was the face of a stranger.

"Hold it, Pete," Steve said softly.

"Give it up," Byrum whispered.

"No. I can't. I won't. Not all that money."

Byrum kept walking, halfway across the room now, toward the gun. Dulaney's mouth tightened. His face changed. In that instant Byrum knew he had gambled and lost. Steve would kill him. But there was no chance to retreat; he had to go forward. He saw the knuckles of Dulaney's hands go white with tension. And then he saw the shadow that suddenly moved in the open door to the patio outside.

Rudge stood there.

"You're both wrong," the man said softly. "Neither of you keeps the money. Because I'm taking it."

Rudge looked as if he had risen from the depths of the sea. His clothes were wet, plastered to his massive chest and shoulders, still dripping small pools of water on the stone floor of the house. A long gash across his face had bled and dried and bled again, untended. The gun in his hand covered them all in the suddenly silent room. His grin was mirthless, his amber eyes like cold yellow stones.

"Put the rifle down, Dulaney," Rudge said. His voice had suddenly resumed the Oxonian accent he sometimes used; he was cool and persuasive. "Don't drop it. I see it's cocked. I'll save you the trouble of pumping a slug into Byrum. I'm looking forward to that job myself. Just lean the gun against the wall like a good fellow, will you?"

Steve's face was pale. He hesitated, then shrugged and carefully balanced the weapon against the wall beside the luggage just inside the doorway. Rudge bent and picked up the briefcase, his eyes on those in the room. Again his gun moved.

"Go on, stand together. Don't try anything foolish, please. I've about had my fill of nonsense from all of you."

"What did you do to Thayer?" Byrum asked. "I'm curious."

"Curiosity will be the death of you, friend," Rudge said.

"Did you kill them both? Serena, too?"

"I never got back aboard," Rudge said. "I'm not much of a swimmer, but Serena and her gun gave me enough stimulus to paddle under the wharf." He laughed. "I still don't know how I did it. I never swam a stroke before in my life."

"You shouldn't have left them," Byrum said.

"Thayer is helpless. He's crippled," Rudge said complacently. "As for Serena, I doubt if she'll give me any trouble." He weighed the briefcase in his hand. "I suggest we all step outside for a moment. This place has its conveniences."

"What—what are you going to do with us?" Myra whispered.

"I plan to even a few scores, Mrs. Thayer," Rudge said. "Getting this money back makes me the fair-haired boy with the New Orleans people, you know. As for your husband, you won't really miss him, will you?"

"You haven't returned the money yet," Byrum said. "You shouldn't have left Serena with her gun."

A flicker of annoyance moved like a small cloud in Rudge's agate eyes. His gun lifted. "What are you trying to do?"

"Warn you, maybe. Serena is right behind you."

Byrum had seen the flicker of shadow moving on the patio beyond the door, not sure if it was simply a trick of the moonlight. No one else in the room had noticed it. Their eyes were fixed on Rudge and on the gun that held them all in paralysis. In the silence, Byrum heard the crash and boom of the tidal surf in the gorge beyond the patio.

Rudge did not turn. "It's a stupid trick, friend," he said.

Serena came into view.

She still had the little gun she had hidden all through the voyage on the *Firefly*. She glided without sound through the doorway and stood directly behind Rudge. Her orange-red hair was tied in a pony-tail again, pulled severely back from her thin face. Her eyes were enormous, giddy with excitement. Her mouth was open, her head tilted to one side.

"Poor Charley," she whispered. "Poor, muscle-bound, stupid Charley. I've wanted to kill you for *such* a long time!"

She fired the gun.

The explosion was small and flat in the room. Rudge was already turning, balanced on the balls of his feet, his massive arm slashing backward at the redheaded girl. His heavy body jerked slightly as the bullet went into his back. But the weight of the small bullet was not enough to check him. His arm smashed down on her gun. She screamed. Byrum leaped for the rifle that Dulaney had leaned against the wall. Steve seemed to be paralyzed by Serena's appearance. Serena fired again, her face twisted, and Rudge stumbled and went down on his knees across the threshold. Serena jumped nimbly back to the patio. Her face was a strange mixture of avid curiosity and hatred. Byrum lifted the rifle and Serena suddenly swiveled her little gun to cover him.

"Don't," she said sharply.

He did not move.

"Get up, Rudge," she said. "Get on your feet."

Rudge wavered to a standing position. His face was gray, his eyes stunned. There were two bullets in him, one in his thigh, one somewhere in his back. Only a small stain of blood showed through his water-stained shirt. He stared in disbelief at Serena as she giggled.

"Outside, Charley. Poor Charley! Step outside."

He whispered something to her that Byrum could not hear. She shook her head. "No. Not at all. Step outside, please."

He walked out onto the patio. Serena flicked a glance at Byrum and the others in the room. "Stay where you are."

Byrum ignored her and followed to the door. The rifle was against the wall where he had returned it when Serena checked him. She had no compunctions; she would enjoy shooting him as she enjoyed shooting Rudge. He could think of nothing more dangerous than challenging Serena Thayer now.

Rudge stood at the railing of the patio, near the gorge beyond. The surf thundered and seemed to shake the very earth on which the house was built. He breathed heavily, his head lowered, his eyes white crescents of rage and pain as he looked at the thin girl with the gun.

"Don't be a fool, Serena," he said. "I never wanted anything except to straighten out the mess your brother made. We can come to terms. But not if you let these people get away."

"They won't get away," Serena said. "Climb over the rail, Charles."

He stared, not comprehending. Serena held her shoulders stiffly, her chin high, the gun leveled at Rudge's stomach. In the moonlight, her face was a death's-head, tight with anticipation.

"Climb over," she said again.

"But I can't swim—"

"I'd like to watch you try. Go ahead."

He hesitated. Her gun abruptly cracked again. Byrum strangled a shout in his throat, took several steps outside, then paused. Serena could see him. He knew she could turn and shoot him as coldly as she had just shot Rudge. The blond man climbed laboriously over the patio rail. The third bullet had gone into his shoulder. His strength must have been enormous.

"Jump!" Serena screamed.

Rudge turned and stared down at the maelstrom below, his face a mask of horror in the moonlight. He looked at Serena and saw the gun twitch in her hand. He jumped.

No one moved. Serena's body was rigid as she stared at the place where Rudge had been. There was no sound from below except the crash of surf on rocks and the hiss of spume as the tide pulled out again. Then, Byrum jumped for her.

He got his hand on her gun. For one more moment, the girl seemed hypnotized by what she had done. Then she turned into a wild, screaming creature in Byrum's grip, trying to free her gun and turn on him. Byrum wrenched it away, slapped her hard across the face. She tried to claw him and he slapped her again. She crumpled suddenly, sprawling in her white dress across the patio stones. He turned and plunged back into the house.

Dulaney had picked up his rifle again. He lowered it as he saw Byrum with Serena's gun.

"I'll take the money now," Byrum said. "You'd better get started for your plane. The next thing I do is call the local police."

Dulaney looked badly shaken by what had happened, no longer the arrogant aristocrat. At a gesture from Byrum, he put down the rifle and picked up the two suitcases.

"Take the rifle, Clemi," Byrum said.

She picked it up as if she knew how to handle it and would use it if she had to. From somewhere outside came a faint screaming.

Byrum said, "You can have your chance, Steve. You can run if you want to."

Dulaney nodded, his face pale.

"I'll give you a start," Byrum said. "Not that I feel I owe you anything." He picked up the heavy briefcase and flipped open the catch with his free hand. The money was there, thick pads of currency crammed inside until the case was filled to the bursting point. He snapped the lock shut again and tucked the money under his arm. "Go ahead, Steve. I'll give you enough time."

"Come with us," Dulaney whispered.

"No. I'm staying here with Clemi."

"They'll pin a rap on you—"

"Maybe. You'd better hurry, Steve."

Dulaney looked at Clemi for sympathy and found none. He touched Myra Thayer's arm and they went outside. A moment later there came the sound of a car starting and then moving off.

Clemi came to Byrum quickly, touching him as if to reassure herself he was real and whole. "You *will* give them a chance, won't you?"

Byrum nodded. "Yes."

"Did Serena—did she kill Rudge?"

Byrum stepped outside. Serena had disappeared, but he was no longer worried about her. Above the thunder of the surf, he heart a faint call for help. He went to the rail and looked down and saw Rudge far below, his head and shoulders out of the water as he clung to a rock, fighting the suck of the tide that threatened to pull him under. The man's face was stubborn, vicious, determined to live in spite of his fall and his wounds. He was still alive, and that was important, Bryum thought. He wanted to keep Rudge alive, somehow.

"Call the police, Clemi," he said. "I'm going down to get him."

Chapter Fourteen

The *jefe de policia* of Guayamas was a man named Ramírez, a slender man with silvered hair and a lean hatchet face that contradicted his dark, limpid eyes. He moved with a lithe grace, tireless after hours on the telephone and after directing his two men, who comprised the entire police force of the village, on various errands.

It was almost dawn. Byrum had lost interest in Ramírez' activities. He was conscious only of a depressing weariness, a need for sleep that dragged his eyes closed for long minutes on end as he waited on the oak chair in the police station. Clemi slept curled up on a bench nearby, a blanket over her. The air had grown chilly in the predawn hours.

The police station was a small musty building on the plaza. Byrum had smoked the few cigarettes left to him and then had borrowed a pack of dark, strong Mexican cigarettes from the *jefe*. There was nothing in Ramírez' attitude to show how the cop felt about him. He was treated respectfully, with reservation, as a *norteamericano,* and Ramírez' English, though stilted and formal, was friendly enough for now. Byrum knew he had telephoned his police superiors in the Mexico City Federal District, and had spoken on a complicated circuit to New Orleans. His senses were dulled. Ramírez had written out a receipt for the money before carefully locking it, briefcase and all, into a small iron safe that stood in one corner of the whitewashed room. Byrum had talked steadily to the cops for over an hour when they arrived at Dulaney's place, but he had carefully avoided any mention of the plane that had taken off only a few moments before Ramírez' arrival.

He slept again as the small square windows of the police station turned gray with dawn. He had no inclination to move. He remembered what he had told Steve. You can't run forever. Some things had to be paid for sooner or later. He wanted it over and done with, now.

"*Senor* Byrum?"

He opened his eyes and saw Ramírez standing before him. It was full daylight now. He felt the heat of the sun on him, pouring through the small windows. Clemi was gone from the bench where she had slept. He asked for her.

Ramírez smiled. His hawk's face looked dark and curious. "There is no need for alarm, *senor*. She is changing her clothes. We found some few things she might prefer to wear to what she had on. It is the eternal woman. She will be back soon. You understand, of course, you are in my custody?"

"Under arrest. Yes."

"In a manner of speaking. Our village is a poor one, but we are fortunate in some respects. Dr. Galvez is a fine gentleman, an honor to his profession. The man you saved from the sea, the one with the bullet wounds—Charles Rudge? —he will live. He has spoken freely. In his terror when he believed death was near, he made a full statement. He is an evil man, a gunman, as you say."

"Yes. He murdered a man named Adam Fahey."

The *jefe* nodded. "To this, he confessed, among other things. You must understand, when you telephoned and turned yourself in to my custody, I contacted Mexico City and New Orleans. I was ordered to hold you for extradition in the matter of the murder of Adam Fahey. This was before *Senor* Rudge spoke so freely, of course."

"And now?"

"The murder charge will be withdrawn. It will be a matter of some time. These things can be complicated."

"What about the money I turned over to you?"

Ramírez spread lean, strong hands. "It is a matter of great confusion, *senor*. It seems to belong to no one. For the moment, it will be held here, pending the decision of your Attorney General."

"You've been in touch with him?"

"A friend of yours, a *Senor* Maury Harris, did so last night. It seems that your disappearance from Oswanda, together with the disappearance of *Senor* Thayer and Rudge, created much confusion in their organization. When the ship appears to sink, the rats will flee, no? Perhaps *Senor* Harris thought it would be a good time to clear his accounts. He signed a full confession as to his activities on behalf of Alton Thayer. There will be a full investigation. We have *Senor* Thayer in custody, too. He is a broken man."

"What about his sister?"

"The strange one? She is in our hospital." The *jefe* shook his silvery head. "She is very ill. Nothing she speaks of is of any sense. I understand she is the one who shot Charles Rudge?

"Yes," Byrum said.

Ramírez nodded. "We know of your recent return from service in your Navy and of your injuries resulting from saving a fellow crewman. Of course, I have orders to hold you for prosecution in your own country for violating the gambling laws in the state where you live. But this surely is not too serious a matter? Especially since through your efforts a far greater case is being made against *Senor* Thayer and the men who supported him. The syndicate, I believe you call it."

"Yes," Byrum said again.

"It may be difficult for you when you return."

"I expect that," Byrum said.

"Well." Ramírez walked to the window and stood looking out at the square and the church beyond. Various sounds drifted in on the hot morning air. The cannery was working and the thump and hiss of machinery together with the clanking of a donkey engine, mingled with the sounds of voices from fishermen on the beach and the tinny blare of a radio in a house behind the police station. Byrum waited. He felt better now. Everything the *jefe* had said held out a hope he had not really expected to find. Maury Harris had finally bowed to conscience and fear and retrieved the ledgers from Thayer's house to turn them over to the authorities. Ramírez had acted quickly and intelligently. What lay ahead was still not known. It would not be easy. He had not expected it would be. But there was hope. He watched the *jefe* turn away from the window, his dark eyes sober.

"One more question, *Senor* Byrum. You can be of great help to us in this affair. We have accounted for *Senores* Rudge and Thayer, with the woman, Serena, who shot Rudge. And we have you and *Senorita* Dulaney. But what of *Senor* Steve Dulaney and Thayer's wife?"

Byrum met his gaze levelly. "What about them?"

"You know where they are? You know where they have fled?"

"Why do you want them?"

Ramírez shrugged. "It has been made clear, since Fahey's body was found in Oswanda yesterday, that *Senor* Dulaney was never guilty of that man's murder. He would have been set free today. With your help, however, he escaped from jail two days ago, stole a boat belonging to Thayer and came here. These are crimes, perhaps of minor consideration against the main picture, but nevertheless they demand answers. Further, they took the money in question from *Senor* Thayer's house and attempted to make off with it. This question must be answered, too."

"The authorities have the money back," Byrum said.

"But not Dulaney or Myra Thayer. Where are they?"

"Gone," Byrum said. "To South America, I think."

"By plane?"

"What makes you think that?"

"I admire your loyalty in seeking to protect them. But we know a private plane was chartered and took off from a cane field near here last night. *Senor* Dulaney was your friend, was he not?"

"Yes, he was. And my partner."

"Then I have sad news for you, *Senor*." Ramírez' narrow face was cool and watchful. "The plane, a Beechcraft, was discovered floating in the sea a hundred miles south of Vera Cruz."

Byrum felt a grayness in him. "Are they dead, then?"

"No bodies have been recovered. The circumstances are peculiar."

"How do you mean?"

"A trading schooner saw the plane come down from a distance of about two miles. The landing on the sea was almost perfect. To the captain of the schooner, the crash seemed to be deliberate, since he had watched the craft come up over the horizon and it was flying normally. Then it circled twice near a small speedboat, and came down to crash. When the schooner reached the scene—it took some time, there was little wind and this was only a native vessel, with no auxiliary engine to help—there was nothing—no bodies, only the empty sea and the plane slowly sinking into the waves." The *jefe* spread his sensitive hands. He smiled thinly. "It is a mystery, is it not?"

"Are they considered officially dead?"

"We must list them so."

"Perhaps it's for the best, don't you think?" Byrum said.

"Perhaps, *senor*."

Byrum wondered. It sounded as if Steve and Myra had

chosen this stratagem to vanish completely. It would be the thing to do to put off both the police and Thayer's syndicate. Perhaps it had really happened that way. Perhaps the schooner people had been mistaken about sighting a small boat at the scene of the crash. Steve and Myra might be dead. He looked at the Mexican, but he could read nothing in the other's dark face.

Let it go, he thought. *You won't see Steve or Myra again. Wish them luck, wherever they are.*

He stood up. "What about my boat? It's tied up at the cannery wharf for now."

"It will be kept safe for you, *senor*. We must hold it in custody for the time being. I am sure, when your personal matters are settled, you will be able to return for it. Until then, I will personally be responsible for its safety."

"Thank you. You're being very kind."

"It is my duty to serve the just and punish the unjust, *senor*."

"Am I free to go now?"

"Within the limits of Guayamas, yes. I expect a representative from your embassy here by noon, to interview you and make arrangements for your return to New Orleans to testify in the case being prepared against the syndicate you have destroyed."

"It's not destroyed yet."

"You have qualms about those people? They will be vindictive against you?"

Byrum said, "I can take care of myself."

"I believe you can, *senor*. I wish you good luck."

He stood outside in the hot sunshine of the square. The iron bell in the church tower tolled nine times, and several black-dressed women and one or two fishermen came down the church steps to go about their day's business. The warm sun and soft sea wind made his weariness fall away. A child went by and smiled at him, and Byrum smiled back. Across the cobblestones of the square, the *posadero* of the inn was sweeping the patio and setting up his tables and wire chairs once more. Byrum was suddenly aware of a desperate hunger. He was halfway across the square when he heard someone call to him.

It was Clemi.

She stood on the steps of the church, just outside the dark nail-studded doors. She no longer wore his shirt and dungarees that had made her look so boyish. With a woman's instinct, she had furnished herself from somewhere with a soft cotton dress the color of gold. It was almost the same color as her hair, which she had combed and coiled into a soft braid. Her shoulders were bare, gleaming a smooth tan in the warm sunshine. He saw her smile and start down the steps toward him.

He felt his heart stop and then beat quicker as he watched her long, free stride, seeing the womanliness of her; and he knew, with humility, that she was dedicated only to him.

She would stand by him; she would wait for him. She would be there when he needed her, when it was all over and a fresh start could be made.

He did not stand there in the plaza waiting for her to come to him. He turned and walked quickly back to meet her.